Prais

'I started reading this with my ten-year-old son ... until he decided the book was so good he had to carry on without me' – Val, NetGalley reviewer

'I loved this book. I did NOT see that ending coming. Five stars and if I could give it more I would' – Amanda W., Amazon reviewer

'A superbly funny debut comedy story ... A wonderful read, full of fun but, above all, heart and a clear message to not give up on your dreams. Perfect for young comedy fans of books by David Baddiel' – Karla, NetGalley reviewer

'This book is great for readers around ten years old, as it has exactly what we like in it' – Toppsta reviewer

ADAM DESTROYS THE INTERNET

Books by Adam B

Adam Wins the Internet

Adam Destroys the Internet

ADAM DESTROYS THE INTERNET

ADAM B

Illustrated by **JAMES LANCETT**

BLOOMSBURY
CHILDREN'S BOOKS
LONDON OXFORD NEW YORK NEW DELHI SYDNEY

BLOOMSBURY CHILDREN'S BOOKS
Bloomsbury Publishing Plc
50 Bedford Square, London WC1B 3DP, UK
29 Earlsfort Terrace, Dublin 2, Ireland

First published in Great Britain in 2023 by Bloomsbury Publishing Plc
This edition published in Great Britain in 2024 by Bloomsbury Publishing Plc

A catalogue record for this book is available from the British Library

ISBN: HB: 978-1-5266-5558-5; PB: 978-1-5266-5559-2; TPB: 978-1-5266-5557-8;
eBook: 978-1-5266-5555-4; ePDF: 978-1-5266-5556-1

2 4 6 8 10 9 7 5 3 1

Typeset by RefineCatch Limited, Bungay, Suffolk

Printed and bound in Great Britain by CPI Group (UK) Ltd, Croydon CR0 4YY

To find out more about our authors and books visit
www.bloomsbury.com and sign up for our newsletters

To my little brother, Callum –

my constant source of inspiration, joy and pent-up-frustration-so-much-so-that-you-always-get-away-with-everything-because-you're-the-little-brother-and-I'm-the-big-brother-and-how-that's-so-not-fair-and-I'd-really-like-to-challenge-the-societal-norms-of-today-but-now-is-probably-not-the-best-time-but-sometimes-you-get-me-angry-grrrr. But no matter what, you're worth it, and may these pages bring as much wonder to your world as you do to mine

1

Flying Ski High

It was a regular Saturday afternoon, just like any other. Not too hot, not too cold, just ... you know, *normal*. And Adam was just a regular thirteen-year-old boy. Not blessed with superpowers, but not totally evil or intent on taking over the world either, just ... you know, *normal*. And currently Adam was in a normal pair of skis, racing down a normal glass roof on one of London's tallest normal skyscrapers. For Adam – Internet Sensation Extraordinaire – this was a fairly normal day.

But it wasn't going to stay that way for much longer.

'WOO-HOO!' Adam cheered as he picked up so much speed that he nearly caused a peregrine falcon to have a heart attack as he zoomed past. 'I have no idea how fast I'm going,' Adam bellowed at the camera that was attached to his helmet, 'but I would estimate that I am travelling at a speed of, approximately … *very, very fast!*'

Then just up ahead he saw something that caused his eyes to widen in alarm. His heart began to race. His visor began to fill with sweat. And his voice trembled as he announced to the millions of viewers who were watching him live on YouTube –

'Erm, guys? I can see the edge of the roof now and … I don't think I can stop!'

Adam was right. He couldn't. At the speed he was pelting down the slope, not even a brick wall would have been able to stop him. But stopping wasn't part of the plan. Adam knew that better than anyone! After all, this whole video was *his* idea. But *planning* to ski off the top of a skyscraper and *actually doing it* are two very different things. And Adam was beginning to wish he'd never come up with such a stupid idea.

'I'm beginning to wish I'd never come up with such a stupid idea!' he screamed at his helmet-cam.

It wasn't even the 'skiing-off-the-top-of-a-skyscraper' thing that scared Adam the most. That was the *easy* bit. It was what was going to happen afterwards that had him quaking in his ski boots. But it was too late for a change of heart now. It was a matter of seconds before he would be hurtling off the edge.

Adam looked directly into the camera and addressed his viewers like a man who was speaking at his own funeral.

'Before I do this, I just have one last thing to tell you. To my mum, to my little brother, Callum, to all of you who have supported me as a YouTuber, I'd just like to say ... WHOOOAAA-ARRRGHHH-EEEEEEE-YEEEEUUUURRRRGHHHH-MMMMUUUUMMMMYYYY!!!'

Adam shot from the roof.

He soared through the crisp blue air.

He flew towards the helicopter that hovered ahead, towards the rope-ladder trapeze that dangled below it, reaching out towards the outstretched arms of Callum, who was dangling upside down from the ladder by his knees, and Adam knew, without a doubt, that their hands were never going to meet. He was going to miss Callum by just a few millimetres, and then … ! Adam couldn't even bear to think about it.

But he didn't have to, because – SMACK! Adam's hands closed around Callum's wrists! Callum's hands closed around Adam's! Adam looked up into his little brother's eyes and screamed with joy – 'CALLUM! WE DID IT!'

And that's when Callum's legs slipped and Adam and Callum Beales, stars of the famous B-Boys YouTube channel, plummeted towards the cold, hard concrete of the London street far below …

But the brothers didn't scream or cry, or go an alarming shade of green, they just stayed like that – arms linked, eyes locked, breathing as one, in perfect unison as they fell. Then together they shouted –

'Three … two … one …'

Like a meticulously rehearsed dance, they released each other's arms, drifted apart from one another, pulled at the handles that dangled from their chests, and – *WHOOOOMPH!* Their parachutes deployed, and calmly and peacefully they drifted down to the street below, where they were met by the cheers and screams of the thousands of fans lining the pavements, all clamouring to get over the barriers that separated them from the paramedics, security teams and reporters who were rushing to meet Adam and Callum as they removed their parachutes.

But someone else got to the brothers first.

'YES!' whooped Ethan, Adam's floppy-haired best friend, as he congratulated them with a pair of almighty high fives before breaking into one of his million-mile-an-hour speeches. 'You should have seen yourselves up there! It was amazing! Adam, you were like *"WHOOSH!"* and Callum, you were like "I got this!" and then it was like "Whoa!" and "Nooo!" and then I thought for sure that you were both gonna die, and then it was like "Yes! They're alive!" and then it was like "No! They're gonna die again! It's gonna be so gross and sticky!" and then it was like "Ahhhh" and then it was like "ARRRRGHHHH!" and then it was like "Doo-di-doo-di-doo, we're just here, floating around in our parachutes like a pair of absolute LEGENDS!" and then it was like "Touchdown!" and then I was like running over to you and I was like "YES!" and "High five!" and "You should have seen yourselves up there! It was amazing!!" And I was like "Adam, you were like 'WHOOSH!'" And then …'

'Ethan!' Adam interrupted. 'We get it! It was amazing! Thank you! We couldn't have done it without you!'

A peanut flew through the air then bounced off Adam's forehead. They all ignored it.

'Seriously?! You mean that?' Ethan said. 'Because I didn't really do anything, to be honest. I just kind of stood around and watched, and then I ate some of those crisps over there, where that guy dressed as a cheetah is handing them out for free, but I don't recommend them because they're *way* spicy, so then I went over to that lady dressed as an alligator to get one of those blue drinks that she's handing out, and it wasn't bad, but probably a bit too blue for me. Do you think it'll make my pee blue? Because—'

'Ethan!' Adam interrupted again as another peanut hit him. On the nose this time. 'Ouch! Look, Ethan, just knowing you were down here supporting us was all we needed.'

'You actually mean that?'

'Of course I mean that. Now, please can you do me a favour? You see over there? Bruce Kilter, the biggest bully the world has ever seen, standing on top of that bin? Holding up a sign that says *ADAM BEALES IS A MORON*? Well, would you mind asking security to take it off him? Or if they could make him get off the bin? Or ask him to leave or something?'

'Why can't school bullies just stay in school?' Ethan lamented. 'Why do they have to bully us from other places too? Like street corners, and car parks, and … bins.'

'Yargh!' Adam yelped as a peanut flew directly into his ear.

'Also, Ethan,' Adam added before Ethan could depart on his mission, 'if you could get him to stop lobbing peanuts at us, that would be a really good thing!'

'On it.' Ethan saluted, did an about-turn and marched towards a pair of burly security guards. 'Attennnnn-tion! Officers! I have a mission for you!'

Adam and Callum could hardly contain their laughter.

'We did it!' Callum exclaimed.

'We so did! And we did it by *ourselves*,' Adam added. 'We did it using our own skills, Callum! I told you we wouldn't need any help from Popularis Incrementum! There is no way the little AI friend who lives in your phone could have made that video any better than it was! Just remember, Callum, if you do ever try to use that Popularis thing, it will not …'

'Yeah, yeah, I know, I know – *Popularis will not solve any of my problems. Popularis will only create MORE problems. Popularis made your life a nightmare last year and* blah, blah, blah! I got it the first time you warned me, *months* ago! And I got it when you warned me every day since then! I got it this morning, when you told me at breakfast! I got it when you warned me at lunch! And I get it *now*. Adam, trust me, I will never try to use Popularis Incrementum. I'm fed up of *hearing* about Popularis Incrementum. And to be honest, I still don't understand what Popularis Incrementum even is! OK?'

Popularis Incrementum – or 'Popularis' for short, or 'Pop' for even shorter, or 'P' for so short it sounds rude – was a bit like one of those voice-activated virtual assistants that do all those random tasks when you tell it to, like 'Play my favourite songs' or 'Tell me what the weather's going to be like tomorrow' or 'Tell me a joke about aardvarks', except Popularis was SO much more than that. Popularis didn't do pointless little tasks, Popularis did HUGE, life-changing tasks. It could literally do the impossible – sometimes when you didn't even ask it to. And nearly always when you least expected it to. And so far it had only revealed itself to one person in the entire world – Adam Beales. Until now. Now Adam's brother, Callum, knew about it too. And Adam was terrified that Callum might try to use it for all the wrong reasons, and mess up their lives, just like Adam had once done.

Adam first realised that Callum knew about Popularis a few months earlier, when, from Callum's room, Adam had heard the strange noises and saw the flashing lights that always came just before Popularis would appear.

'Your computer started squealing, right?' Adam panted when he had arrived in Callum's bedroom doorway and found him sprawled across the floor, looking extremely confused. 'Like BEEEEEEEP! And then the screen started getting brighter and brighter, and then FLASH! FLASH! FLASH! It felt like it kicked you in the brain, and you found yourself on the floor, right?'

'How did you know?' Callum had replied as he sat himself back at his desk.

'Because the same thing happened to me once, Callum! A message came up on my computer, promising to make all my dreams come true, like there was some kind of magical genie living in the internet – it called itself "Popularis Incrementum". But what it didn't tell me was that it would also make my worst *nightmares* come true!'

'But … like … are you saying that it *did* make some of your dreams come true? Was it like a competition? And you won?'

'No! Callum! You're not listening! It's nothing like that! It was like *magic!* It gave me this riddle, it was written in a boxy old font that looked like it had time-travelled direct from the 1990s, and that riddle led me on a quest, and I thought it was so cool! And every now and then, without any warning, I'd hear that high-pitched BEEEEP again, and see flashing lights from my phone, or a camera, or a TV, and then something *impossible* would happen! And, at first, it was awesome! But then things started to go wrong, and then I wished I'd never gone anywhere near it in the first place, so that's what I'm telling you to do – stay away from it.'

'I don't get it,' Callum had muttered. 'Are you explaining a *dream* you just had?'

'No, Callum! This was real, this was … forget it. You don't need to understand it. All you need to know is to stay away from Popularis Incrementum. It doesn't mean any harm. It really is only trying to help. But it *will* mess things up. It will ruin your life!

And … at some point … you will probably dance around in a nappy, with thousands of people laughing at you.'

'OK!' Callum had quickly agreed. 'I'm convinced! I'm never going anywhere near it!'

But Adam wasn't sure that Callum did understand. And he also wasn't sure that Callum was telling the entire truth, because every now and then Adam could have sworn he saw Callum on the internet, searching things like '*Popularis Incrementum, send me on a holiday to Disneyland*', or he would be on his phone, sending emails to someone, and giggling to himself and whispering things like 'I've always wanted to be able to fly!' Adam even once caught Callum crouching in front of the TV, saying, 'If you can hear me, I want you to do my homework for me!' Of course, Callum insisted that Adam was being ridiculous, and that he had been asking the TV to play a show called 'Do My Homework for Me.'

But Adam had been pretty sure that Callum was lying. He had a sneaking suspicion that Callum was still trying to get Popularis's help with something. And he had a horrible feeling he knew exactly what Callum would be asking Popularis to do for him …

A team of people were helping to get Adam and Callum free from their parachute harnesses, when a huge grin spread across Callum's face.

'Hey, Adam, do you think this could be the one? Do you think this could be the video to get us up to ten million subscribers? I mean, we already got our Silver Play Button award for reaching a hundred thousand subs, and our Gold Play Button award for reaching one million, but do you think it could actually push us all the way to *ten million*? Think about it, Adam – we could actually get a *Diamond Play Button award!*'

Adam didn't share any of Callum's excitement. He took a deep breath and put a brotherly arm around Callum's shoulder.

'Callum, how many times do I have to explain to you – it's not about how many views or how many subs we get. It about *having fun*. If all you think about is the numbers, you will become obsessed, and that will *not* be fun. Trust me, I've already been there.'

'I know, I know, but I'm not getting obsessed, honestly!' Callum insisted, still bouncing with excitement. 'But you have to admit, it would be cool, wouldn't it? I mean, a *Diamond Play Button*, Adam! It's, like, the ultimate prize! Well, no, I suppose the Red Diamond Play Button would be the ultimate prize. But I'm not being fussy! The Diamond one would be *amazing*! It would be a dream come true! My ultimate wish!'

Adam's arm dropped away from Callum's shoulder, and his expression became so serious his face almost turned to stone.

'Dream come true? Ultimate wish? Callum, you have to promise me you will *not* try to use Popularis to mess with our B-Boys channel! We cannot risk messing it up! It has to be just the two of us! No one else!'

'Ugh, Adam, just because I said "dream" and "wish" doesn't mean I was thinking of summoning your weird internet fairy! They were just words! Not everything is about Popularis Incrementum,

OK? I'm beginning to think *you're* the one who's obsessed!'

Adam's stony expression finally cracked, and a smile shone through.

'You're right. Sorry, Cal.'

Adam and Callum were just about to make their way over to meet some of their screaming fans when someone else caught their eye – a very wobbly, green-tinged somebody, who looked as though they needed a lie-down and a cup of tea.

'Mum! You OK?' asked Adam, rushing over to her.

'Oh, me? Erm … Of course! Never better!'

'Are you sure?' asked Callum. 'Because you look like you might be *sick*.'

'Me? Sick? Sick with *pride* over you two, maybe!'

'Did you see us? Did you see it *all*?! Did you see the bit with the helicopter? I wish Dad could have seen us too,' said Adam, suddenly going misty-eyed.

Adam and Callum's dad had died a few years earlier, and they missed him every day. But they missed him EXTRA on special occasions like birthdays, holidays and skiing down London's tallest skyscraper days.

'Do you think he'd have been proud too?' Adam asked his mum.

'I *know* he would be! He always was. Knowing my luck, he would have probably wanted to join in!'

Adam and Callum both laughed at the thought of their computer-nerd dad skiing down a skyscraper, but then something his mum had said stopped Adam, mid-laugh.

'What did you mean when you said "knowing my luck"?'

'Oh, nothing, just, you know, well …'

The rest of Mum's sentence was cut short by a chant that the fans had begun, and which was getting louder and louder with every call.

'B-Boys! B-BOYS! B-BOYS! B-BOYS!'

'Go on!' Mum chuckled, shepherding Adam and Callum towards the fans. 'I think a few people over there might want to meet you!'

So Adam and Callum cheerfully headed over to meet their fans, pausing on the way for some press photos and doing a bunch of silly poses for the cameras.

Adam gave Callum a celebratory high five.

'Here's to making the impossible possible, all by ourselves!'

'Definitely!' agreed Callum. 'And who knows, maybe a Diamond Play Button award might be the next impossible thing we win!'

Adam gave Callum the beady eye.

'But you really *won't* try to use Popularis, will you?'

'No way, Adam! Of course not! A promise is a promise! Not for this, not for trying to win the Lottery, not for *anything*!'

But as they made their way over to meet the fans, Adam could have sworn that, behind Callum's back, he saw his fingers looking a tiny bit ... extremely ... completely ... *crossed*.

2

The Problem

On the plane back home to Derry, Adam was supposed to be using his brain to think up new ideas for their next big video, but his brain wasn't paying attention. All Adam's brain could think about was ...

WERE Callum's fingers crossed when he told me he hadn't been using Popularis, or did I just imagine it?

And ...

If he HAS been using Popularis, what has he been using it for? Did he use it on our stunt today? Our last video? ALL of our videos??!!

And ...

Something big and horrible is going to happen because of this, I just know it!

In the car, driving home from the airport, Adam regretted beating Callum in their race to the front seat. *If I was sitting behind him, I'd be able to see what he's doing on his phone. I BET he's trying to contact Popularis right now.* Adam used the windows and mirrors to try to get a peek at Callum's screen, but it didn't work, plus he was distracted by the way his mum kept wiping her eyes.

'Mum? Are you *crying*?'

'No,' said his mum, smiling as she sniffed back more tears. 'It's fine. I'm fine. I'm just being silly.'

She wasn't telling the truth and he knew it.

'What's that saying you're always telling me and Callum? *A problem shared is a problem halved?*'

His mum groaned and laughed and sighed all at the same time.

'Well done, Adam, bouncing my own saying right back at me! I suppose you're right. Yes, something is troubling me, but it *is* just silly, and nothing you need to worry about. It's just … when you and Callum were up there, dangling from the helicopter, I was so scared I was going to lose you, just like we lost your dad, and … well, that's it really.'

'And you're still crying about it?' laughed Callum. 'That was *hours* ago!'

'Callum!' Adam snapped, maybe sounding a little more cross than he had meant to. 'It's not funny! Can't you see Mum's upset?'

But the truth was, Adam had thought exactly the same thing – how could she still be crying about *that*?

'But we're fine now,' Adam reasoned gently. 'We were safe the whole time, and we didn't get hurt, so … you don't need to be sad.'

'I know,' his mum said with another soft laugh.

'But I guess it *really* scared me, that's all. But I feel better now for talking about it. You were right. A problem shared *is* a problem halved. Thank you.'

She reached across and squeezed his hand, which finally gave Adam an idea for their next video.

Instead of just doing videos to make our subscribers happy, we're going to do a video to make MUM happy, just in time for her birthday next week.

Perfect.

The only problem was, Adam had no idea what that video might be.

Perhaps I could ask Callum to ask Popularis for a little help with …

NO! Adam was furious with himself for even *thinking* it!

No more Popularis ever again! And that includes Callum!

Adam resolved to find out, once and for all, if Callum really was using Popularis, and if he was, what he was using it for.

So, that night, when Adam and Callum had both gone to bed, Adam decided to stay awake, and when Callum fell asleep, Adam would sneak into his room, take his phone and hunt down any traces of Popularis.

But it wasn't quite as simple as that …

No matter how long Adam waited, Callum just never seemed to go to bed!

At 11.16 p.m., Adam peeked out of his bedroom door, but Callum's light was still on.

He's definitely up to something. That sneaky little rat! He NEVER stays up this late!

At 1.49 a.m., Adam crept up to Callum's door, just to check that Callum hadn't fallen asleep with the light on, but, through the tiny crack of Callum's almost-but-not-completely-shut door, Adam saw Callum, still wide awake, still sitting at his desk, still furiously typing away at something on his computer.

Trying to contact Popularis, I bet! He's such a liar!

Then at 4.08 a.m., a noise woke Adam up. He groaned as he achingly stood up from where he'd fallen asleep, sitting on the floor, leaning against the wall, next to his bedroom door. He wondered how long he'd been asleep for, and then he heard it again – a creaking floorboard, out on the landing. Once again, Adam peeked through his doorway and straight across the landing to Callum's room. Adam's heart leaped with surprise to see that Callum's bedroom light was *still* on, but his door was now wide open. Quickly and silently, Adam crept across the landing and peered into Callum's room, only to find that there was no sign of Callum.

Weird!

And no matter how hard Adam searched, there was no sign of Callum's phone either.

Double weird! He usually has his phone plugged in, charging, all night long.

He switched Callum's computer on and scrolled through all the open windows. Not a single trace of Popularis to be found. No internet searches, no strange ads saying, 'Click here to make your dreams come true!' Just games, videos and cooking websites with recipes for birthday cakes.

Triple weird!

Adam was beginning to wonder if he had been wrong about Callum all along. Maybe he hadn't seen him crossing his fingers yesterday. Maybe it was all in his imagination. Heading back out of Callum's room, Adam switched off the light, and something strange immediately caught his eye. There, beneath Callum's desk, sitting in his printer tray, was a small stack of paper that was *glowing*. Adam instantly flicked the light back on, grabbed one of the pages from the printer tray, and his mouth fell open in amazement at what he saw.

'Gotcha!' he whispered.

There was no mistaking it. It was *identical* to the first message Adam had ever received from the mysterious internet genie – the same scrawled handwriting, the same rhyming kind of riddle, the same ridiculous 1990s graphics. Everything about it was *exactly* the same except for … every single word that was written on it –

To succeed in your mission, you must go to the top
Explore what's on offer, and don't ever stop
The answer's in Harrington, what you wish you must speak
Only then shall you win the prize that you seek

(Now please stop bothering me. I am the world's most advanced artificial intelligence, and you're using me like some child's plaything! Come back when you have something less time-waste-y to challenge me with! Until then, I'd appreciate it if you would leave me alone, as I have a few thousand *really* difficult crossword puzzles I'm trying to finish! Yours sincerely, Popularis Incrementum)

And just like the riddle Adam had once received from Popularis, this one also made

ABSOLUTELY
NO SENSE
AT
ALL!

But this did answer everything Adam had wanted to know – Callum had definitely been using Popularis, and had *definitely* been lying to Adam about it! And those last few words of the riddle gave Adam the feeling that he knew exactly what Callum had asked for – *Only then shall you win the prize that you seek.*

'A prize ...' Adam whispered to himself. 'He *is* using Popularis to try to get a Diamond Play Button! I knew it!'

And this made Adam furious! Made Adam feel like he could never trust Callum again! Made Adam feel like sharing the B-Boys channel with Callum was the worst decision he had ever made! And when he got hold of Callum he would tell him all of this to his face! But before he could do that, he had one more question that needed answering –

Where on earth IS Callum?

Adam stepped out on to the landing. No light coming from downstairs. Nobody in the bathroom. No ... wait. There was *something* in the bathroom ... a *ladder* ... going up into the loft.

Of course! That's where Callum is! thought Adam. *He's following the riddle.*

Adam looked at the glowing page in his hand –

To succeed in your mission, you must go to the top

Adam couldn't decide whether Callum's idea to literally go *to the top of the house* was total genius or totally stupid. But, remembering how Popularis's riddles liked to say one thing but mean another, he guessed that it was stupid. Callum did tend to do the most stupid things possible. There's no way the riddle could be that simple. But, as far as Adam was concerned, this was good news. The more Callum got it wrong, the better. The last thing they needed was any of Callum's ridiculous wishes to be granted, and for a whole load of internet-related chaos to come crashing down on them as a result.

Adam decided it was time to go up into that loft and stop all of this before it got out of hand. But when he got up there, once again, Callum was nowhere to be found. But the bare light bulb at the other end of the loft was still swaying back and forth on its cord – a clear sign that Callum had been up there just moments earlier. And beneath the swinging light bulb was a single box, with the lid torn off. And as Adam approached it, he noticed the logo printed on the box's delivery label – 'Just Keep Going! Derry's fastest parcel delivery.'

'No way!' Adam gasped. 'It can't be …'

He looked back down at the riddle in his hand, this time to the second line –

Explore what's on offer, and don't ever stop

'Just keep going … Don't ever stop … They mean the same thing!' Adam whispered to himself. 'And he came up here to *explore* – *explore what's on offer* and … Don't tell me the little idiot's actually getting this riddle *right*?'

The box was completely empty, all except for a single envelope, clumsily ripped open. The envelope was also empty, but the paper had shaped itself around the outline of whatever had been inside it, and Adam tried to figure out what it might have been. Something long and rectangular.

'A highlighter pen? An eraser?' he whispered to himself.

But Adam stopped trying to guess the contents when he noticed that the envelope had an address scribbled on the front of it –

Mr H. Beales
Office A21, Harrington Industries

Harrington Lane
Harrington Industrial Park
Derry
BT47 9XY

Adam looked back down to the last two lines of the riddle and instantly felt sick.

The answer's in Harrington, what you wish you must speak
Only then shall you win the prize that you seek

'He's getting it all right!' Adam gasped in horror. 'Each clue is leading straight to the next! It's so simple! All he has to do is go to this Harrington address, say his wish out loud and it'll come true! I have to stop him!'

Just then, Adam heard the unmistakeable CLATHUNK of the front door closing. He rushed to the loft window and looked down just in time to see Callum slipping out into the golden sunburst of dawn, still dressed in his SpongeBob pyjamas, which matched perfectly with the yellow case of his clunky old brick of a phone. He was holding the phone in one hand and a peculiar-looking device in the other. Adam squinted, struggling to get a clear look at the contraption. He couldn't make out what it was, but it was about the size and shape of a highlighter pen, or a long eraser, but Adam knew it was neither of those, because this thing had a flashing red light on top.

Adam's instinct was to bang on the window and yell for Callum to stop, but he knew that if he did, two bad things would happen:

1. Callum would know Adam was on to him, and would probably make a run for it
2. He would wake Mum up, and she would stop him from doing what he knew he had to do next – *follow Callum and stop him. Before it was too late.*

3

Follow the Yellow
Brick Phone

'Being a private investigator wasn't an easy job. The hours sucked, and the pay was even worse. But I wasn't in this game for the money. I did it because it was the only thing I knew. Being a PI was in my blood.'

Adam was outside, pressed flat against a wall. Hiding while he filmed himself on his phone. He was worried and tense, and as usual filming always made him feel happier, even if nobody would get to see the content, so he was attempting to turn his hunt for Callum into some kind of dramatic manhunt. But less usual was the soft American drawl he spoke in, as if he were adding his own voice-over to one of those old detective films, and he was the star. The cooler than cool investigator. The cooler than cool investigator who was wearing superhero PJs, and had a serious case of bed hair.

He took a quick glance around the edge of the wall, down an overgrown alley, saw the distant yellow glow of Callum disappearing around a corner, then cautiously slunk after him.

'I was on the heels of a lowlife scumbag, but this time it wasn't just some dime-store hood or some sorry schmuck who was cheatin' on his dame – this time it was personal. I'd been double-crossed by my own partner.'

Adam slowed as he reached the corner where he'd just seen Callum disappear, peeking around it just in time to see him climbing a mesh fence into a scrap metal yard.

'The one person in the world I thought I could trust,' Adam continued, persisting with the accent. 'I treated that kid like a brother. And then he repaid me by stabbing me in the back. And he thought I'd be fool enough not to notice. Dumb schmuck.'

Adam waited for Callum to be far enough away not to hear him following, then he scurried towards the fence and began climbing it himself.

'What he didn't take into account was ... Ow, sheesh!' Adam suddenly fell out of character as he slid back down the fence. 'How did he get over this thing?'

Adam tried climbing it again. And again. And again. And after many more 'Ow!'s and 'Sheesh!'s and 'Yow, that's SPIKY!'s, he finally made it to the other side, and jumped back into character.

'Luckily my years of training kept me spry and limber, able to tackle any obstacle that came my way, and – Arrghh! HEDGEHOG!'

Adam quickly ducked behind a rusted old car as Callum whipped round to see where the noise had come from. Adam peeked around the side of the car and saw that once Callum was confident he was on his own he carried on, following a map on his brick-phone. And once Adam was confident that the tiny hedgehog wasn't going to tear him limb from limb, he stepped over the little thing and hurried to keep up with Callum.

'It was like a game of cat and mouse. I wanted to catch that scumbag in the act. I needed to see it with my own eyes to truly believe it, and I needed proof of his guilt if I was going to take him down. But if he got even just a whiff of my scent and knew I was on his tail, it'd all be over. Luckily all my years as a PI had taught me how to blend in, disappear, be as stealthy as a fox, as silent as the – WAAAAHHHH!'

Adam walked straight into an antique lawn-mower, stumbled into a sheet of corrugated steel, then landed flat on his face in the long grass.

He stayed there. Perfectly still. Completely silent. Not even breathing as he heard Callum turn round and call out, 'Hello? Is someone there?' He waited a long time before he lifted his head, ever so slightly, and peeked through the long grass to see if Callum was still looking. He wasn't. It was much worse than that. He was *gone*.

Adam jumped to his feet and began racing in the direction Callum had been heading.

'No!' he whispered to himself, not bothering with the accent any more.

He reached the end of the scrap metal yard,

clambered up the fence and looked all around, into the miles and miles of wasteland and derelict buildings that surrounded him. But Callum was nowhere to be seen.

'NO!' he hissed as he jumped down, over the other side of the fence, and continued running straight ahead.

Adam was in a part of Derry he had never seen before. He was passing through places he never knew existed. Past abandoned factories, empty car parks overgrown with weeds and shrubs, through half-completed building sites, now swamped in waist-high grass. He was sprinting, panicking, and there was still no sign of Callum!

'No, no, NO!!!' he growled in frustration.

What if Callum had already found the address from the envelope? What if he was already saying his wish out loud? What if Popularis was about to mess their lives up at that very moment?

Adam tried to remember the address so that he could put it into the map on his phone, so it could lead him to where Callum was going, but there was no point – his phone was out of battery!

'NO! NO! No-no-no-no-*NO*!'

Then a boost of hope quickly lifted Adam's heart when he suddenly found himself on a road. A road which, like everything else around him, was completely empty and long abandoned. But, most importantly, it was a road with a sign, a sign that read *Harrington Lane*.

'This is it!' Adam whispered to himself. 'This is the street from the envelope!'

Now he *knew* he was on the right track. All he had to do next was go to the next part of the address – the building.

What was it called? Harrington Ltd? Harrington Inc.? If only I'd brought the envelope with me!

He raced down the road, hoping to find a building name that might jog his memory, and he didn't have to go far. The entire road was lined with old, empty buildings. Old, empty buildings, which, like the road, looked brand new, yet were covered in years of dirt and vegetation. And there it was, just two buildings down to the left – a huge, glass-fronted office block, with a bold sign above the entrance –

And just above that sign, on the other side of a huge window, was the yellow glow of Callum's phone as he trudged slowly up a long flight of stairs.

Adam almost leaped with joy.

He's still on his way in! He hasn't done it yet! There's still time!

He wanted to scream and wave and do everything he could to get Callum's attention, to stop him from doing what he was about to do, but he knew that would only make Callum go even faster, to finish his quest for the Play Button before Adam could catch up to him. So Adam laid himself down on the weed-covered pavement and hid behind a pile of lamp posts, until Callum reached the top of the stairs and disappeared from view.

Adam leaped to his feet and ran as fast as he could. He sprinted across to the building, threw open the doors, darted inside and began bounding up the stairs as quickly and silently as he could before slowly slipping through the same doorway he'd just seen Callum go through.

Adam stopped dead in his tracks. He was standing in a huge, state-of-the-art, ultra-modern concourse that looked more like the lobby of a fancy hotel than part of an office block. But, in contrast to the sleek surroundings, the roof was a total mess. A tree had apparently fallen on it some time ago, allowing daylight, rainwater and all the rest of nature inside. Small trees were sprouting up from the floor. Ivy was growing up pillars and beams. And birds were happily flying around in the roof space. Then something snapped Adam out of his goggle-eyed state of wonder – up ahead, in one of the offices, someone switched a light on.

Adam raced towards the office, ready to stop Callum, ready to catch him red-handed! But then he froze. Something felt wrong. What if it wasn't Callum in there? *What if someone has lured Callum here? Like a trap.* Adam himself now felt like a mouse being led towards a chunk of cheese, and that any second now a trap would spring on him. He looked around for a weapon, and grabbed the only thing he could find – a small, fake, dust-covered plant, sitting in a pot outside a nearby toilet. Then, slowly and bravely, he poked his head into the office.

Adam gave an almighty scream and jumped back just microseconds before a toilet brush came slamming down in the exact spot where his head had just been. Adam scrambled back so fast that he fell on his butt, and began furiously crawling backwards, away from his toilet-brush wielding attacker who leaped into the open doorway with his weapon held aloft.

'AAAAAARGHHHHH!' the attacker roared with almighty triumph. 'AAAAAAAAAAA … dam? What are you doing here? Did you *follow* me?'

'Callum! You absolute idiot! What are you attacking me with a toilet brush for?!'

'Well, why are you carrying a plastic tree? I saw your reflection in the computer screen and thought you were a ninja with a sword!'

'Callum,' Adam said, trying to catch his breath as he clambered back to his feet, 'I know exactly what you're up to, and you have to stop! Right now!'

'No, but, Adam, you don't understand! I ...'

'I *do* understand, Callum! You've been using Popularis! After you promised me you wouldn't! You're using it to try to get your hands on that Diamond Play Button, and I couldn't be more ashamed of you! You're selfish, and you're greedy, and you're shallow, and you're a LIAR!'

'Adam!' Callum yelled back, red-faced and furious. 'Why don't you EVER listen to me! I'm trying to explain to you that ...'

'I don't listen to you because all you do is LIE! How can I believe a word that comes out of your mouth when you're so obviously keeping so many secrets from me?!'

'Oh, sure, like I'm the only one who keeps secrets round here!' Callum shot back. 'Well, if using Popularis is so bad, how come you never tell me anything about it? You never tell me *why* it's bad, you say, "*Ooh! No! You mustn't use it because it made me sad once! Boohoo!"* Well, guess what, Adam? I'm not a little kid any more! I can figure things out for myself! And if you're not going to listen to me –' Callum reached into his pocket and pulled out his own glowing printout of the riddle, and held it in front of Adam's face – 'then I'll do *this* by myself too!'

The office door slammed in Adam's face, and then there was a CLICK! as Callum locked it from the inside. And then, from way up in the huge roof, there was an ominous groan as one of the huge steel beams bent a little further under the weight of the huge dead tree that lay across it.

Adam looked down from the roof and swallowed hard. He stood there, stunned. Stunned because Callum had *never* spoken to him like that before. Stunned because, well, Callum was right – Adam had been keeping secrets from him. He had never explained the details of how Popularis had messed his life up, or how Popularis had been invented by their *dad*, and that, sometimes, when you spoke to Popularis, it almost felt as if it was Dad talking back to you. And finally he was stunned because, as he stared at the office door in front of him, he realised that he hadn't been the only one to keep secrets – the nameplate on the door read: *Office A21, Harry Beales, CEO, Harrington Enterprises*.

This was DAD's business?

He was the BOSS here?

I never even knew this place EXISTED!

Why didn't he ever tell me?

Why didn't MUM tell me?

Why didn't …

Adam's confusion was interrupted when he heard Callum muttering to himself on the other side of the door. Except it wasn't himself he was talking to. Adam knew exactly what he was doing – he was telling his wish to Popularis!

The answer's in Harrington, what you wish you must speak
Only then shall you win the prize that you seek

'CALLUM, NO! DON'T SPEAK IT! YOU DON'T KNOW WHAT YOU'RE DOING!'

Adam pounded on the door, causing the roof beam to creak and groan some more.

'CALLUM! UNLOCK THE DOOR! I THINK SOMETHING BAD'S ABOUT TO HAPPEN!'

But Callum didn't reply.

'CALLUM!' Adam bellowed.

The roof gave an almighty yawn, followed by a BOOM! And huge chunks of roofing panel rained down over the concourse, causing birds to shriek and fly for cover.

'CALLUM! WE HAVE TO GET OUT OF HERE! OPEN THE DOOR! NOW!'

And when Callum still didn't reply, Adam decided to take things to the next level. He stepped back a few spaces, took a run-up towards the door, then threw himself at it, shoulder first. The door burst open and Adam went careening in, colliding with a desk opposite.

Callum didn't even flinch. He just stood there, phone in one hand, toilet brush in the other, with a look of immense disappointment on his face. And as Adam picked himself up from the floor, rubbing his aching ribs, Callum slowly turned to face him.

'Don't worry, Adam, it didn't work,' he muttered numbly. 'I did what the riddle said, but it didn't work. Nothing happened.'

'Callum! We have to go! This place isn't safe!'

'Wait! I forgot!' Callum's eyes widened as he reached into his pyjama pocket and pulled out the pen-like object with the blinking red light that Adam had spied from the loft window.

But Adam now had a clear view of exactly what it was – a memory stick.

'I bet I need to plug this in!'

Adam made a grab for him, but missed as Callum rushed over to a computer, plugged the memory stick in and waited for it to power up.

'CALLUM! WE HAVE TO GO!'

But Callum wasn't listening. Within seconds, the computer was on and a high-pitched, brain-piercing *BEEEEP* was coming out of it.

'NO!' Adam roared.

The screen began to glow a blinding white. Brighter … brighter … *brighter!*

'CALLUM, DON'T!' Adam pleaded.

Then –

'Popularis ...' Callum began.

He paused to look up as a humungous branch broke off the dead tree above and landed with a crash, directly outside the office door, blocking their way out.

FLASH! went the computer screen.

'Popularis ...' Callum repeated, but Adam jumped in –

'POPULARIS! GET US OUT OF HERE!'

By now the whole building was beginning to shake!

'NO!' wailed Callum. 'I have to make my wish! Popularis, keep us here!'

FLASH!

'NO!' Adam barked. 'POPULARIS! WE HAVE TO GO!'

Chunks of roof were raining down all around them, smashing windows, crushing desks ...

'NO, POPULARIS! WE HAVE TO STAY!'

'GO!'

'STAY!'

'GO!!!'

And then it happened – the bent and twisted

49

beam above them snapped in half, and a chunk as long as a bus went hurtling towards them, and …

FLAAAAASSSSHHHH!

The beam went crashing down on to the office, crushing everything inside it, just as, in a blinding explosion of pure white light, Adam and Callum disappeared into thin air.

4

Lots of Screaming

The little bald man wearing little round glasses was quietly sitting at his desk, drawing doodles of chickens in shining armour and innocently biting into his egg salad sandwich when, all of a sudden, Adam dropped out of nowhere and landed in the corner of the office. In his pyjamas. Holding a fake plant. Looking confused beyond belief. The little bald man almost fell off his chair with shock, when something else caught his attention – Callum's big, round face appeared out of nowhere, so close to him that their noses were almost touching. The terrified little man stared into Callum's bulging eyes. The terrified Callum stared back at the little man. Adam stared at *everything* in utter bemusement. Callum gave a small yelp. The man gave a startled whimper. Adam gave a dumb-founded 'Huh?' And then, out of pure terror, Callum bopped the little man on the nose with his toilet brush and started screaming like a goat on a roller coaster. The little bald man clutched his little bald nose and started screaming like a man who'd been bopped on the nose with a toilet brush. And then Adam started screaming like ... a *really confused Adam*!

Screaming seemed to be all the rage in office A21, and it went on for quite some time. It's under-standable really. Most people who were about to be completely flattened by a falling piece of roof, then inexplicably found themselves in a completely different place altogether, would most likely do at least a little bit of screaming.

And then Adam *stopped* screaming. Looking around the office, he got the feeling that maybe they *weren't* somewhere completely different. This office looked remarkably like the one they had just been in. Except this one was clean, with a ceiling, and an added little bald man, and ... oh yeah, it hadn't been completely flattened by a gigantic piece of roof! But other than that, it was the same. The same, but … *different*. And because Adam had stopped screaming, Callum stopped too. And so did the little man. They all stared at each other. They caught their breath. The little bald man looked as if he was about to say something. And then the door burst open. A spindly old lady in a spindly old suit stepped inside to see what all the screaming was about. She glared at Adam and his deadly, fake plastic plant. She glowered at Callum with his fully loaded toilet brush. She set her jaw. She folded her arms. She opened her pinched little mouth and said –

'AAAAAAAAARRRRRGHHHHHHHHH!'

And that started the whole thing off all over again.

Adam screamed. Callum screamed even louder. The little bald man screamed until he actually did fall off his chair. And, as Adam and Callum escaped from the room by crawling between the spindly old lady's spindly old legs, she screamed so hard she passed out.

And as the brothers screamed, they *ran*. They ran

across the concourse that looked exactly the same as the one at Harrington Industries. The same, but *different*. They ran down the stairs and out through the same front doors. The same, but *different*. And leaving a trail of screaming office workers in their wake, the screaming escapees ran on to the same Harrington Lane that they had arrived on. The same, but *different*. The weeds were gone, the lamp posts were up and the sign on the side of the road no longer read *Harrington Lane* but *STEPHINGTON Lane*!

They ran and they ran, confused and screaming, one carrying a toilet brush, the other carrying a plastic plant, both wearing pyjamas, away from the unfathomable weirdness behind them and towards the same Derry sunrise that had been with them all morning. The same, but ... *different*.

Adam had no idea what on earth had just happened, but he had a very good idea of who was behind it ...

'Popularis!' Adam yelled towards the sky. 'What have you done?!'

But Popularis did not reply.

And when their throats had grown hoarse from screaming, and their legs had turned to jelly from so much running, they paused for breath on a bench, in a park they'd never seen before.

'Callum. Phone. I need it,' Adam demanded, lowering his head between his legs as he caught his breath.

'Use your own! My battery's only on twenty-eight per cent.'

'I can't! My battery's on *zero*.'

'Charge it up when we get home. I'm using mine to call Mum. Tell her to pick us up before someone from school sees me walking around in my pyjamas.'

'Pyjamas?' Adam scoffed. 'We almost got killed by a gigantic piece of roof, we just got transported to … I don't even know where, we're probably the first humans ever to teleport, and you're worrying about your *pyjamas*?'

'Yeah, sure, all that other stuff was freaky, but it's over now, right? Look, there's St Eugene's Cathedral, there's City Hotel, there's Columb's Park – everything might be messed up back *there*, but it all looks normal over there, so I say let's forget about the messed-up bit, and let's head back to where it's normal.'

Adam hated to admit it, but Callum was right. Something weird had definitely just happened, and they couldn't really ignore that, but, for now, heading home was probably the best option. Besides, now that he thought about it, Adam wasn't too keen on being spotted hanging about in a park in his PJs either.

'Well, what are you waiting for? Call Mum!'

'Ughhh,' groaned Callum. 'No signal. We'll have to keep walking.'

So, reluctantly, the two brothers picked themselves up and began trudging back towards home, the *long* way, obviously. There was NO WAY they were going back down Stephington Lane, or anywhere near that weird office block ever again.

'The second Popularis gets in touch with you again, you better tell him to fix whatever mess you two just created, because whatever it was that just happened back there, it was all because you were messing about with Popularis when I warned you not to.'

'*Him?* You call Popularis a *him*? It's not a human, Adam, it's an AI. Or an OS. Or something.'

Again, Adam felt guilty for still not explaining how Popularis seemed to have a little bit of their dad in it. But now wasn't the time for that conversation.

'Anyway,' Callum continued, 'whatever happened back at the office was because *you* were messing around with Popularis, crying at it to *get us out of here! I want my mummy!*'

By the time they got home, Adam and Callum were too exhausted to notice that there was something about their house that was decidedly ... *different*. The same, but different. They didn't notice the perfectly manicured flower beds out front. They didn't notice that their front door was a gleaming, bright white, rather than a dirty, greyish-brownish white. They didn't even notice the whopping great extension on the side, which made their house nearly twice as big! It was only when they strolled in through the front door that they began to realise that things weren't quite right ...

'Whoa! Mum's taken the hall carpet up! Who

knew we had these fancy tiles underneath?' remarked Callum, giving the shiny floor tiles a tap with his toilet brush.

'Hah! And she's finally taken down our stupid school photos! Yes!' exclaimed Adam as he admired the fancy new painting that was hanging where the photos used to be.

In fact, it wasn't just the school photos that had gone – *all* the family photos were missing. And so were the coat pegs! No coats, no school bags, no collection of Callum's endless hoodies that he never put away. There was just a single peg, with a fancy designer jacket he'd never seen before, and a brand-new, sparkly handbag. In fact, the more Adam looked around, the more he noticed how every one of his and Callum's belongings had disappeared. Almost as if they had been completely wiped from existence. And it didn't end there. When the brothers got to the kitchen, their jaws practically hit the floor.

'What the … how is our kitchen *so big*?' Callum gasped.

'And what happened to our *garden*?' added Adam, as he gazed through the brand-new bifold doors, out at the luxury landscaped paradise outside.

But at least there was *one* thing that was still familiar in the house —

'Mum! I'm so glad to see you! We've had such a messed-up ... *Whoa!* Since when is your hair *brown*?' puzzled Callum as he stared at his mum, who was sitting at a shining new breakfast bar, with a coffee in one hand and a croissant in the other, and a look of utter terror hanging from her face.

'Eghck!' she spluttered.

'Mum? You OK?' asked Adam. 'Your face has gone completely white!'

'Guh!' she gasped as she jumped to her feet.

'Are you cold?' asked Callum. 'Your hands are shaking!'

'G-g-g-geh!' she stammered.

'Did we do something wrong?' enquired Adam. 'Only you look kind of ... *furious.*'

Adam quickly ducked as Mum's coffee cup went flying towards his head.

'WHOA!'

Callum opened his mouth as wide as he could as Mum's croissant went flying towards *his* head.

'FANKSH!' he cheered through a mouthful of pastry.

And then their mum finally managed to form an actual word. Five of them, in fact.

'GET OUT OF MY HOUSE!!!!'

Her ashen face instantly turned purple, and she began a non-stop onslaught of random-object-lobbing at the boys – a plate, a book, a biscuit, a *stool*.

'HEEEELLLLLPPPP!' she shrieked at the top of her voice. 'INTRUDERS!'

And the screaming started all over again.

5

Inter NOT

Mum did a lot of screaming. Like, *loads*. Adam and Callum had never heard anything like it! At first they wondered if she was throwing things around in celebration, and screaming with relief that they had finally returned home after disappearing while she had been asleep. But that, very quickly, proved not to be the case. Then they wondered if she was screaming because she had taken part in a TV show where they come round and do your house up, all posh and fancy, and try to surprise the rest of the family when they get home, and Adam and Callum had arrived home too early and ruined the surprise. But that wasn't the case either. Neither was she screaming because she'd stubbed her toe, seen a terrifying burglar standing directly behind Adam and Callum, or because all the bins were overflowing thanks to Adam forgetting to take the recycling out four days earlier.

No, it turns out that the reason she was screaming was because:

1. She had no idea who Adam and Callum were
2. She desperately wanted them to get out of her house
3. She seemed to think that they might have been spies. Or aliens. Or alien spies.

They figured all of this out from something their mum had said while screaming and throwing stuff at them. It went a little bit like this –

'AAAAARGHHHH! HELP! WHO ARE YOU? GET OUT OF MY HOUSE! HELP! SPIES! ALIENS! ALIEN SPIES! HELP! GET OUT!'

And that's when she called the dogs. Two of them. Big ones. Dogs they didn't own, had never owned and never would own!

So, just like back at the offices, the screaming had been followed by running. Lots and lots of running. And even more running once they'd heard the police sirens heading their way!

Twenty-eight minutes later, Adam and Callum had finally made it to safety. They were panting for breath, drenched in sweat and sheltering in the best hiding place they could find – a hedge. At the side of a road. Not too far from the park they'd found earlier on.

'Whooh!' sighed Callum, wiping the sweat from his eyes. 'And I thought that stuff in the office was going to be the weirdest thing to happen to us today!'

'And I've got a horrible feeling that this is just the beginning,' Adam groaned, clutching a stitch in his side.

'But *what* is just beginning, Adam?!' Callum whispered. 'What's happening? How did that roof not crush us? How did we magically appear somewhere else that was … the *same place*? Why didn't Mum recognise us? Why did she set those evil ponies on us? Why did she call the police? Why did our house look so different? I don't get it! None of it makes sense!'

Adam wasn't quite so frantic. He was mostly annoyed. Angry. With a clenched jaw and flared nostrils. Staring out at the passing cars.

'I have one answer for you, Callum – Popularis Incrementum! I told you not to mess with it! I warned you, over and over again. I specifically told you never to try to use it to mess with our B-Boys channel, but you still went and did it! And now look what's happened! You broke the *world*!'

'I'm sorry, Adam! I didn't mean to! But I *promise* you I wasn't doing anything to mess with our channel or …'

'Callum, when will you stop with the lies? I know exactly what you were using it for! I saw the riddle from Popularis! You wanted to win your "prize"! And we all know what prize you've been after since the day we set up our channel – the Diamond Play Button! And how do I know that? Because it's all you ever talk about! So please, enough with the lies, just tell the truth for once!'

Now it was Callum's turn to look angry. He sat there, not saying a word, biting his tongue until he couldn't hold it in any longer and the rage spilled out of him like anger-flavoured vomit.

'OK! Fine! You want to know the truth? You want to know what I really asked Popularis for? I asked him to help me—'

'Shhhh!' hissed Adam as a police car slowly rolled past, with its windows down, and Mum in the back seat, searching all around for the intruders who'd broken into her house.

'Would you recognise them if you saw them again?' one of the officers asked her. 'Could you describe them for us?'

'Evil-looking.' Mum shuddered. 'Strange clothes, almost like pyjamas. The big one was holding a plastic plant. The other had a toilet brush in his hand, and a … a strange gadget, like alien technology, like a small window that glowed with lights and pictures. I'm telling you, they were either spies or from another planet, but they definitely weren't from round here!'

The car rolled away, and the brothers allowed themselves to breathe again.

'How does she not even know what a *phone* is?' Callum whispered. 'What have I done? I … I … I know it *is* my fault for messing with Popularis, even if I wasn't doing what you think I was doing. And I wish I could fix it all, but … I don't even understand how I broke it!'

'Well, you *did* break it, Callum,' Adam sighed, wrapping his arms around his knees and resting his head in the crook of his elbow. 'And now our mum doesn't know who we are, and you're sitting in a hedge, in your pyjamas, with a *toilet brush in your hand!*'

'I still don't have any signal, which is weird,' said Callum, checking his phone again. 'But if we can just get on to a computer I'll see if I can get hold of Popularis, and ask to put everything back to normal, I promise, Adam.'

'Ughhh, Callum, you still don't get how Popularis works! He doesn't come when you *call* him! He comes when he feels like it! It's not like he's your servant and you're in charge! That's the whole problem! You're *never* in charge! Popularis is! Popularis is *always* in charge!'

'Except … that's not entirely true, is it?' said Callum. 'Because he *did* come when I wanted him to, back at the office, he came as soon as I plugged *this* thing into the computer.'

Callum reached into his pyjama pocket and pulled out the pen-like memory stick with the flashing red light on top.

Adam plucked the memory stick from Callum's fingers and stared at it in amazement.

'How did you even get this back, Callum? How did you possibly have time to take it back out of the computer before the roof fell in?'

Callum swallowed hard as he realised – 'I *didn't*.'

'Popularis wanted us to have this with us. *He* gave it back to you! This thing must be important, Callum. It has to be! But what is it?'

'Look!' said Callum, snatching the memory stick back off Adam. 'There's something written on it!'

 Callum turned the memory stick over in his hand to reveal four letters scrawled across it in black marker pen.

'P.I.S.C.,' he read aloud. 'What do you think that stands for? Plug ... Into ... Special ... Computer? Particle ... Initiator ... Santa Claus?'

'That doesn't even make any sense,' sighed Adam, snatching it back off Callum. 'S.C. stands for source code, the building blocks of something, the original design. And P.I. has to stand for ... Popularis Incrementum! Callum! This *is* Popularis! The very first design! The original hard copy! That's why Popularis appeared when you plugged it in! Popularis is *in here!*'

Callum's eyes were as wide as his gaping mouth.

'So ... you mean ... we just need to plug that thing back into a computer, and Popularis will appear again, and we can tell it to put everything back to normal?'

'Yes! And we can ... Oh. Except ... there's just one problem.' Adam groaned in disappointment. 'Our computers are in our house, and we can't get into our house because it's being guarded by police and two of the biggest dogs in existence!'

'Those were *dogs*?! Are you sure they weren't angry horses?'

'Callum, try to focus.'

'No, OK, sure, yeah. A computer. We'll just use another one. Easy!'

'And where exactly are we going to magically get our hands on another computer? Ask Mum if we can borrow hers? I don't think that's going to work!'

Callum scratched his head, as if he was literally trying to pull an idea out of there. Then a thought came to him. But it wasn't the thought Adam had been hoping for.

'Adam. If that memory stick is the Popularis source code, then ... why was it in a box, in *our* loft, addressed to *our* dad?'

But Adam didn't get a chance to finally explain, because that's when they heard a voice approaching. A very familiar voice, rattling away at a million miles an hour, and the answer to their computer problem revealed itself ...

'... And so I was like – "Whoa! *Watermelons!*" And she was like – "Nuh-uh!" And I was like – "Oh yes." And then Mr Lee sticks his head through the window and he was like – "Have you seen five guinea pigs passing through here?" And we were

like – "What?" And he was like – "Never mind."
And then he gets practically knocked over by, like,
twenty cops and some lady screaming "ALIENS!"
And that's when my grandma fell through the
ceiling, so …'

'ETHAN!' Adam and Callum yelled with joy as
they leaped from the hedge.

Ethan jumped so high with shock that he
spun around in a full circle and landed on
his bum.

'WHOA! No! Please! I don't have any money!'
Ethan wailed, covering his head with his arms and
curling into a ball.

'Ethan!' Adam laughed. 'Relax! It's *us*.'

Ethan peeked out from between his elbows. He
looked at Adam, then to Callum, then the clunky
old phone in Callum's hand, then he snapped his
elbows shut again.

'It's *you*,' he squealed. 'The ones the lady was
shouting about! You're the ones who attacked her
with a toilet brush, and …'

Ethan peeked back out to look at Callum's
phone again, which seemed to fascinate him for

some reason, the way racing cars on TV seem to fascinate cats. And then he lowered his arms and had a proper good stare at it.

'What *is* that thing?'

Callum blushed and hid his shabby, yellow, outdated phone behind his back.

'It's just Callum's old brick. Mum won't let him get a new one.'

Ethan eyed Adam suspiciously.

'That's not a brick. It's made of *glass and metal*. Do you think I'm some kind of idiot?'

'No, I didn't mean an actual "brick",' Adam tried to explain. 'I meant … are you *messing* with us?'

'No! I'm sorry!' Ethan crawled backwards slightly, as if he were afraid that he'd offended Adam somehow. 'I didn't mean to mess with you, it's just … Where are you *from*?'

'We were just in the hedge!' Adam explained. 'We didn't mean to jump you. It's just that everyone's acting so weird, and …'

'And the police are searching for you,' Ethan added for him.

'Well, yeah.' Adam shrugged, looking ashamed. 'But we didn't attack anyone! You see, it's Mum! Something's happened to her, and she …'

'You didn't answer my question,' Ethan butted

in, growing more confident and getting to his feet. 'Where are you from? That lady said you were, like, spies or …'

'We're not aliens, Ethan!' Adam laughed. 'It's *us*! Adam and Callum!'

'Adam and Callum …' Ethan said the names as if testing them out in his mouth. 'Are you, like, famous or something?'

Adam and Callum looked at each other and shrugged.

'Kind of,' said Callum. 'A little bit.'

'Not *internationally*,' added Adam. 'Not really.'

'Except in India,' Callum corrected him. 'We have a lot of subscribers in India.'

'Well, that's true,' Adam agreed. 'And Canada too, I suppose. And Lithuania, weirdly. They really like our channel in Lithuania.'

'Do you really not know us?' Callum asked, sagging with disappointment.

'Subscribers, you said?' muttered Ethan, rubbing his chin curiously. 'So, are you, like, in … publishing? Magazines, or something?'

'YouTube!' Adam laughed, causing Ethan to

jump back in fear once more. 'Ethan, we're YouTubers! Do you really not remember?'

Ethan frowned at them as though he was waiting for any of what they'd just said to start making sense.

'Tubas? Like … you're in a *brass band*?'

'What?' spluttered Callum, who was also frowning as if waiting for *Ethan* to start making sense.

'Please don't tell me you haven't heard of YouTube,' groaned Adam.

'I haven't got a single clue what either of you are saying right now,' Ethan admitted. 'And you're weirding me out, big time!'

Adam accidentally poked himself in the eye with his plastic plant as he attempted to bury his face in his hands.

How can this be happening? he asked himself. *How can it be real? My mum and my best friend have no idea who I am! Popularis! Why are you doing this?!*

Adam took a deep breath. He tried to calm himself. To stop the world from spinning. And then he tried again.

'OK,' he said to Ethan, slowly and calmly. 'I'm

sorry if we scared you. And we didn't mean to weird you out, it's just that, well, we're pretty weirded out too, and we really need your help.'

'Why me?' Ethan asked, still sounding nervous. 'Why *my* help? How do you even know who I am?'

'Well, this is going to sound *really* strange, but ...' Adam took another deep breath. 'Yesterday you were my best friend. We've *always* been best friends. You know everything about me, and I know everything about you, like ... your mum's called Sally and your dad's called Tony, you had a cat called Galileo, but he disappeared last year, and never came home.'

The look of astonished disbelief on Ethan's face told Adam that he was getting somewhere. It was working! So Adam carried on, quicker.

'You, err, your favourite ice cream is pistachio, and that really annoys you, because nowhere sells it. You're obsessed with space and all things science-y. You ... you, err ... oh, yes! You have a big birth-mark on the back of your right thigh, a mole on your right shoulder that has big, gross hairs growing out of it, a scar on your little finger on … I can't remember which hand, but it's from when Ben Portland swung his anorak at you and the zipper caught your finger, just above the nail. Your favourite author is Jules Verne, you're obsessed with multi-level video games, and your favourite show is *Tom and Jerry*. I have no idea why.'

Ethan stared at Adam for a long time, seemingly speechless.

'Am I right?' asked Adam.

'Err … yeah. Kind of. All except the multi-level viddy game thing. And I've never been to see any Jerry and Tom show. The last show I saw was *Dick Whittington*. And I hated it. But, yeah. Everything else was … How did you *know* all of that?'

'I told you,' said Adam. 'We're … we *were* best friends.'

'OK, sure. Right. And … so … what do you want from me now?'

'We just really need to borrow your computer!' Adam pleaded. 'I swear you can trust us! We don't even have to come into your house. You could just bring it out to us. For two minutes. That's all we need. And then we can fix everything that's gone wrong. *Please*.'

Something happened to Ethan's mouth that almost looked like a smile, then he said – 'That's it? You just want a go on my *computer*?'

'Please!' Adam repeated.

Ethan paused to think about it, then finally nodded.

'OK. But I have two conditions.'

'Anything!' Callum blurted. 'We'll do *anything*.'

'Well, first of all, you'll need to leave your weapons here.'

Adam and Callum looked at each other, brows furrowed with confusion, and that's when they realised they were still holding the plastic plant and the toilet brush.

'Done!' they both exclaimed, tossing their 'weapons' into a nearby bin. 'What else?'

'Secondly, my best friend is coming with us,' Ethan declared.

Adam looked momentarily hurt when he realised that Ethan wasn't talking about *him*.

'Err … yeah, of course! Who is your best friend?'

Ethan pointed over Adam's and Callum's shoulders, and now it was *their* turn to jump out of their skins as they realised that, standing directly behind them, this whole time, was Ethan's friend. Silent, staring and completely still, right up until he gave a tiny wave and muttered – 'Hello.'

Adam was dumbstruck. He could hardly believe his eyes. Just when he thought his day couldn't get any stranger!

'*Bruce?*' he blurted in a weirdly high-pitched voice. 'Your best friend is Bruce "The Biggest Bully in the World" Kilter?! Are you serious?'

'Bruce isn't a *bully,*' Ethan corrected Adam. 'He's, like, the nicest guy *ever.*'

'But he *hates* you! And *me*! And he … he … stands on bins and throws *peanuts* at people!' Adam insisted.

'I really don't,' Bruce informed him politely. 'That would be mean, not to mention extremely negligent of the fact that so many people suffer severe and life-threatening allergies to peanuts. I would *never* do such a thing.'

Adam was a little bit shocked. He'd never heard

Bruce utter anything that was so … *sensible*. Adam wasn't quite sure how to reply, so he simply muttered, 'Well, you did it *yesterday*,' and he rubbed his nose as he remembered the pain from Bruce's peanut attack.

'So, how do you think my computer's going to fix your problem?' asked Ethan as he began leading the way towards his house.

'I think we've gone back in time,' said Callum, 'so I guess it'll just send us back to our time.'

'Callum,' said Adam, in his very best 'Are you a complete idiot?' voice. 'If we've gone back in time, why is Ethan still the same age he was back home?'

'I dunno, sheesh, so maybe we've gone *forward* in time!'

'Erm, again, Callum. Ethan – still the same age. If we'd gone forward in time he'd be older, don't you think?'

'OK, fine, Mr Smartypants, what's your genius theory?'

'My theory is that you used Popularis when you shouldn't have, and messed up our world, and wiped us from existence!'

'That's an interesting theory,' Ethan commented, 'but …'

'It's a contradiction of quantum entanglement,' interjected Bruce, still trailing behind as they walked on.

'Exactly, Bruce! You're a genius!' cheered Ethan. 'What Bruce is saying is that, if what you were saying is true, and yesterday you existed but today you don't, then that wouldn't stop the rest of us from remembering who you were *yesterday*. Unless … yeah, I suppose our memories could have been wiped, so that we don't remember *anything* before today. Except … I *do* remember yesterday. Crumpets for breakfast. Yellow wee because I didn't drink enough water. Double science in the afternoon – *awesome*. I remember *everything*. I remember breaking my arm four years ago. And eating three portions of jelly and ice cream at Katie Pike's eighth birthday party. And throwing up jelly and ice cream all over Katie Pike's mum. Possibly too much information. But the point is we all have histories in this world. And you two were never part of them. Nor were your weird glass-and-metal brick things.

So I don't think your theory makes sense. You *can't* have existed yesterday. Not *here*, at least.'

'I don't understand any of what you're saying right now,' admitted Callum.

'Interdimensional teleportation,' explained Bruce.

'Exactly, Bruce! You're a genius!' Ethan cheered again. 'What I'm saying is this – have you considered the possibility that you might have been transported to an alternate dimension? A parallel universe, where it still *seems* like your world, except there are small differences here and there?'

Adam thought about this as he looked around the houses they passed in Ethan's neighbourhood. Almost everything looked exactly the same as it always did. But only *almost*. Mr Lafferty's front garden was now decorated with dozens of miniature windmills instead of the garden gnomes he'd been collecting for years. Mrs Algrove was making her routine trip to the corner shop, but instead of being led by Clarence, her guide dog who she'd had since she lost her sight six years ago, she was cycling down the road, at top speed! And, at the end of

Ethan's road, the big red letterbox with a huge dent in the side from where Shannon Tingle had reversed into it during her driving test was now dent-free and as good as new.

'Everything's the same,' Adam whispered to himself, 'but *different*.'

'So you think we've jumped to an alternate universe, where the only difference is that nobody knows who me and Adam are?' scoffed Callum. 'Doesn't seem likely, does it?'

'Wait ...' muttered Adam, as if an amazing idea had just fallen into his head. 'That *does* make sense! Callum, what was the last thing you said to Popularis before we got zapped away?'

'I don't know.' Callum shrugged. 'Something like, "Keep us here, Popularis, don't listen to my big brother being a crybaby and wanting to go home."'

'Close enough,' agreed Adam. 'And what was the last thing I said to Popularis?'

'That you wanted to go home because you're a big crybaby?'

'Exactly! Apart from the crybaby bit. I told Popularis to take us away. You told Popularis to keep us here, and it did as we *both* asked — it kept us in the same place *and* it took us away! Callum, Ethan and Bruce are right! Popularis has transported us to an alternate universe!'

'But, if we're in an alternate universe, why are Ethan and Mum here?' asked Callum.

'Interdimensional fluctuations,' explained Bruce.

'Exactly, Bruce! You're a genius!' Ethan cheered for a third time. (It really did appear that Bruce actually was a genius!) 'That's how alternate universes work,' Ethan explained to Adam and Callum. 'There could be *trillions* of alternate universes, each with a world exactly like ours, except for one tiny little difference. For instance, there could be a world identical to ours in every way except that blue is called red and red is called blue. Or where cats go woof and dogs go miaow, or …'

'Or where dogs are horses and horses are dogs!' Callum butted in.

'Ugh, Callum,' Adam groaned, 'for the last time, those *were* dogs!'

'It all makes perfect sense,' Ethan continued. 'You've come from an alternate universe where …

can we call it an altiverse? That sounds so much cooler, right? An *altiverse*. I like it! Anyway. You've come from an *altiverse* where, unlike this one, people carry glass-and-metal bricks with them, there's some magical genie called Poppy Lawrence or something, and where you two *exist*, and where people use *computers* to travel between dimensions.'

'Well, actually, as far as I know, no one else has done the interdimensional transportation thing before,' Adam admitted. 'Just us.'

'And now, in order to get back to your universe, you want to do it *again*?' said Ethan, sounding unconvinced.

'Correct,' said Adam.

'You want to do it *here*, in this universe, where there are no magical genies and interdimensional travel doesn't exist?' asked Ethan, sounding *really* unconvinced.

'Correct,' said Adam.

'And you think you'll be able to do this with *my computer*?' asked Ethan, sounding as unconvinced as it's possible to get.

'Correct,' said Adam.

'But not *just* your computer!' Callum explained. 'We're going to use *this* too!'

Callum whipped out the memory stick and held it out for Ethan to see.

'OK, that makes a lot more sense. That *does* look pretty awesome and sci-fi. It even has a flashing red light thingy on the top and everything,' said Ethan, finally sounding as convinced as can be. 'Well, let's give it a go and see what happens!'

They had finally reached Ethan's house, and were about to follow Ethan inside when the door slammed in their faces and Bruce piped up nervously from behind them.

'I'm guessing you don't have VZs in your universe, correct?'

'What is a *VZ*?' asked a very baffled Callum.

'I'll take that as a no.' Bruce chuckled before pointing over to the left of the front door, to an empty porch-like area, built around a small, cupboard-sized hatch in the wall. 'A Visitor Zone.'

'A *what*?' said Adam and Callum in unison.

'Are you telling me that people in your universe

let other people *inside their homes*?' asked Bruce, sounding utterly horrified.

'Well, yeah,' said Adam. 'Not just *anyone*, but if you know them or trust them, why not? Are you saying that you've never been in Ethan's house?'

'Why *would* I?' gasped Bruce. 'That's his personal space! That would be so messed up!'

The hatch in the wall suddenly slid open with a loud *THUNK,* and Adam and Callum leaped back in shock.

'Here we go ...' said Ethan, who was only visible from his waist to his shoulders through the small opening in the wall, as he passed something out to Adam, '... one computer!'

Adam stared at it.

Callum stared at it.

They both felt instantly sick.

'That's ... not a computer,' Adam muttered.

'Er ... yes, it is,' Ethan assured him.

'No, Ethan, *that* is an abacus. An ancient counting device made from beads and wires. We need a *computer*. A machine, with a screen, and keys, and a brain that figures things out for you!'

'Ohhhhh! OK, don't worry. I think it's just a name thing. We call *this* a computer,' explained Ethan, pointing to the abacus. 'What *you're* talking about is –' Ethan ducked down behind the hole in the wall and came straight back up to hand something else to Adam – 'a *calculator*.'

Adam stared at the object.

Callum stared at the object.

'No,' said Adam. 'That's not a computer either. That is a calculator. We need a *screen*. A big screen. A monitor. And the internet. With a keyboard!'

'A keyboard ...' repeated Ethan. 'Are you sure you're not in a band?'

Adam slumped to the floor of the VZ. Callum slumped next to him.

'We're definitely in an altiverse,' Adam said with a note of horror in his voice.

'An altiverse where we don't exist,' agreed Callum, sounding equally horrified.

'And worse than that, neither do phones, computers or ... the *internet*!' groaned Adam as he pulled the Popularis memory stick from his pyjama pocket. 'Which means that this thing is completely useless! Which means that ...'

Adam couldn't bring himself to finish the sentence, so Callum did it for him –

'We're stuck here!'

6

Order Boxes, Cuddle Gnomes and a Possible Way to Get Back Home?

Adam and Callum were not taking the news about being trapped in an alternate universe with no way of getting back home especially well. They did lots of clutching their heads, and pacing round Ethan's garden, and muttering things like, 'This can't be real' and 'This can't be happening' and 'This can't be … I think I'm going to be sick!' And then they did some sitting down and burying their heads in their hands and groaning things like, 'There has to be a way' and 'There has to be an answer' and 'There has to be … I really am going to be sick!' And then they started doing really weird stuff like bashing their heads against the door of Ethan's VZ, and slapping themselves on the cheeks while wailing things like, 'I can't breathe!' and 'I'm so dizzy!' and 'I really am going to be … Bleurghh! Bleurghhh! BLEURGHHH!'

And Ethan and Bruce weren't being much help. Ethan did bring out a huge box of tissues, except these ones were called 'Tear-sues', which Adam didn't really use. And then he brought out another box, which Callum didn't use either. And then he

brought out a stuffed toy for Adam, except he called it a 'Cuddle Gnome', which mildly resembled a garden gnome, except it had long, spring-loaded arms that wrapped around your neck, and which confused Adam almost as much as the news about being in an alternate universe. And then Ethan brought out another Cuddle Gnome for Callum, which Callum did gratefully tuck under one arm. But then Ethan and Bruce mostly just stood there, staring uncomfortably, until, eventually, when Adam and Callum had finished almost-but-not-quite being sick, Bruce finally offered some words of comfort …

'I'm hungry. Anyone else hungry?'

'Good thinking, Bruce,' said Ethan, giving his friend a high five. 'I'll see what's for dinner.'

Adam and Callum's wailing and moaning subsided while they watched in confusion as Ethan disappeared into his house and came back out with a newspaper in his hands.

'OK, let me just get to the Dinner page … Aha! Right, so for dinner today, we have – number one: spaghetti bolognese, number two: fish and chips, or number three: curry and rice.'

'I don't think I want anything,' muttered Callum as, finally dipping into the Tear-sues, he dried his eyes. 'I just found out that I'm never going home agai— Wait, did you say *fish and chips*? I might be able to manage fish and chips.'

'Me too, I suppose,' added Adam. 'Hang on, you have your food options printed in a *newspaper*?'

'How else would we find out what's for dinner? Don't tell me that in your universe you still have someone ringing a bell, calling out the dinner options on every street corner? That is SO old-fashioned!' Ethan laughed. 'We, my friends, have moved on. This is meal ordering for the twenty-first century! So, two fish and chips ...'

'Make that three!' added Bruce.

'OK, four fish and chips it is! Let me just check ...'

Ethan poked his head in through the VZ hole in the wall.

'MUM! DAD?'

There was no reply.

'Good. They're still at work. Let me grab the doodah ...'

Adam and Callum watched closely to see how exactly Ethan was going to order this food, both of them wondering, *hoping*, that Ethan might pick up some kind of phone.

If they have phone lines, they might at least have something that resembles *the internet!* Adam thought. *That's how the internet started, after all — sending information down phone lines!*

Adam's eyes lit up as Ethan reached back and pulled out a grey box, the *actual* size of a brick, with a big coiled wire attaching it to something inside the house. It looked like a cross between the massive walkie-talkies Adam had seen in old cop movies and an old-fashioned house phone. He couldn't contain himself. He had to see for himself! He snatched the device from Ethan, pressed the green button, held it to his ear, then spoke into it.

'Hello?' he said.

There was no sound other than Ethan and Bruce trying to stifle their laughter.

I must look like an idiot! I didn't even dial a number!

Adam looked at the face of the grey box. Below

the big, round, green button were three big, round, white buttons, numbered one, two and three.

Only three buttons? I guess their phone numbers are pretty short here!

Adam punched in a random number – 1322.

'Wait! No!' Ethan protested, reaching out a hand to stop Adam pressing the green button, but he wasn't quick enough.

Adam put the box back to his ear.

'Hello? Is anybody there?'

Ethan and Bruce could not contain themselves. They exploded in hilarity, clutching their stomachs and actually rolling on the floor in laughter.

'He thinks there's a little man inside it!' Bruce managed to howl.

'A little chef, waiting to take his order!' added Ethan, barely able to breathe from laughing so hard.

'That's the funniest thing I've ever seen!' Bruce screamed, turning purple in the face.

Adam and Callum watched on as the laughter continued for what seemed like a completely unnecessarily long time, until, finally, Ethan and Bruce managed to compose themselves, and sat back up.

'I'm guessing you don't have Order Boxes in your universe,' Ethan chuckled, taking the grey box from Adam's limp hands. 'I suppose that's one area where we're a bit more advanced than you.'

'I don't get what's so funny,' said Callum.

'There is no little man in the box, waiting to take your order,' giggled Bruce. 'It's connected by a wire, direct to the Meal Kitchens. You type in the number of your order, and they deliver it to your house!'

'Meal Kitchens?' said Callum. 'Not a restaurant?'

'What's a *rest-runt*?' asked Ethan.

'I don't think they eat out in the altiverse,' Adam told Callum.

'We do,' Bruce corrected him. 'We eat in our gardens, when the weather's nice.'

'And this box ... it's *just* for ordering meals?' asked Adam.

'Uh-huh,' confirmed Ethan. 'And instead of ordering four fish and chips, which would have been number two, four times, you ordered one spaghetti bolognese, two fish and chips and one curry and rice – one, three, two and two. And I am *not* having the curry and rice! *Way* too spicy!'

Adam finally let himself laugh at his mistake.

'Ethan back home doesn't like spicy food either,' he chuckled.

'Look! He's actually smiling!' said Bruce, pointing a finger in Adam's face.

Adam flinched. Still not used to this alti-Bruce, Adam half expected a peanut to come flying out of Bruce's hand. But it didn't.

That still doesn't mean you can trust him, Adam reminded himself. *Bruce can do a pretty good job of* pretending *to be nice back in our universe too.*

'See, it's not that bad here!' Bruce continued. 'I mean, there must be worse universes to be stuck in. You never know, you might even *like* it in our altiverse!'

'Exactly!' added Ethan. 'I mean, we don't have glass-and-metal bricks, or your computers, but we do have some really cool stuff, like, we have these things called "bikes" and "scooters" and ... and there's this *game*, it's so cool! And you'll love it! It's called *Monopoly*!'

'Yeah! And we have brilliant food too!' Bruce chipped in. 'We have this one thing – you have to try it one day – it's called *pizza*!'

'And don't forget,' said Ethan, with a reassuring smile, 'just like in your dimension, we still have tubas and keyboards, so it's not all that bad!'

Adam's laughter instantly died away as the reality of their situation returned to him.

'But we don't have a home here, do we?' he muttered. 'Or a *mum*. We don't have *anything* here. Not even the internet!'

'Well, I don't know what the inter*net* is, but we do have something called the InterNAL, which sounds like it could be similar,' said Ethan reassuringly. 'Well, we almost do. Some science boffin at Stephington just invented it.'

'The *InterNAL*?' gasped Adam. 'That does sound kind of like the inter*net*! Maybe it's the same concept! Maybe we could use it to get Popularis up and running again! We need to speak to these people! What do you know about this InterNAL thing?'

'I know that it's supposed to completely

revolutionise NAL communications,' began Ethan, as he gleefully recalled every piece of information he'd ever read on the subject. 'I know that it's going to be the next big thing, and everyone is going WILD about it. I know that it's being developed *right here*, in Derry! At Stephington Industries!'

'Whoa! Wait! What?' spluttered Adam, struggling to process so much information at once. 'What is "NAL communications"? And … *Stephington Industries*? Is that the company on Stephington Lane?'

'You know it?'

'We went there this morning,' explained Callum. 'And we didn't make a very good first impression. I don't think they'll be falling over themselves to welcome us back.'

'Well, I guess if you want to go back there, you're going to need disguises,' suggested Bruce. 'Preferably ones that make you look less like kids. And if we can come up with a good cover story, I can probably get you an interview with the guy who invented the InterNAL.'

'*What?*' laughed Adam. 'Are you serious?!'

'Yeah,' said Bruce, shrugging it off. 'I kind of

know someone who works there, so it shouldn't be a problem, except that, well, science boffins usually only have meetings with other science boffins, not, erm, little kids in weird circus outfits.'

'These are *pyjamas*! Why is everyone so confused by that?' lamented Callum.

'Those are *pyjamas*?' laughed Ethan. 'Well, science boffins don't have business meetings with little kids in pyjamas either. Especially bright, colourful ones like those!'

'So, yeah, disguises,' said Adam. 'And we'll need to come up with a good excuse to set up a meeting with him. Something he can't refuse.'

So that's what they spent the rest of the evening doing – hiding out in Ethan's garden shed, trying out different disguises, eating fish, chips, spaghetti bolognese, curry and rice, coming up with ideas for a fake business meeting, and having way too much fun in the process.

'Guys!' hissed Ethan. 'We have to keep our voices down! My parents are back from work and they'll absolutely *lose it* if they find out I've got friends round! We are breaking so many rules right now!'

'Sorry,' the others all said at once.

'I can't get used to this whole "no-socialising" thing you've got in this altiverse,' whispered Adam. 'It's, like, the complete opposite of our universe.'

'I've got it!' Callum whispered excitedly, accidentally spraying bits of fish from his mouth. 'An idea for a fake meeting! Why don't we just tell him about Popularis, and how we're the first people to do into-the-men-channel travel?'

'Firstly, it's *interdimensional* travel,' said Adam. 'And secondly, because we want to tell him something *believable*, Callum. Otherwise we may as well tell him that we flew here on magical, rainbow-eating unicorns.'

'Why don't you pretend to be inventors too?' said Ethan, holding a huge lab coat in front of Callum, to see if it would fit. 'Say that you've invented a new kind of abacus, using keyboards and tubas!'

'Yeah,' sighed Adam, trying on one of Ethan's dad's tiny suits and drawing a moustache on his lip. 'I don't think that's going to work. We need to know more about this guy.'

'Do some research on him,' suggested Bruce,

throwing Adam a copy of *Business Weekly*. 'There's a whole article on him in there.'

Adam flicked through the pages until he found the article titled '*InterNAL to Revolutionise NAL Communications*', and his heart did a little leap of excitement in his chest.

'I've got it!' declared Ethan. 'Why don't you just tell him about the inter*net* thing, from your universe?'

Adam looked at the picture of the scientist responsible for developing the InterNAL, and his heart did a little backflip of anticipation.

'Tell him how the whole thing works! Tell him you invented it!' Ethan continued.

Adam looked at the caption below the scientist's photograph, and his heart did a

TRIPLE SOMERSAULT OF AMAZEMENT!
A LOOP-THE-LOOP OF UTTER DISBELIEF!
A FIREWORK EXPLOSION OF '*OH-MY-WHAT-THE-HOW-CAN-THIS-POSSIBLY-BE-REAL?*'-NESS!!!

The caption was just nine words. Nine simple words that would change the rest of Adam's life …

**Tech-wizard inventor of the InterNAL,
Professor Harry Beales**

'You could even tell him …'

'Tell him he's our DAD!' Adam cheered as he jumped to his feet.

'Erm … no,' said Ethan.

'That would be really weird,' agreed Bruce.

'Super weird,' added Ethan. 'The unicorn idea was better than that.'

'No!' laughed Adam. 'He IS our dad!'

Adam's eyes filled with tears as he pulled Callum to his feet and thrust the magazine under his nose.

'It's DAD, Callum! Dad's here! And he's *ALIVE*! Look!'

Callum stared at the magazine with his mouth hanging open.

'Huh?'

'Callum, OUR DAD IS ALIVE IN THIS ALTIVERSE!'

7

Off to Meet the Tech Wizard

'I can't believe how quiet it is here!' Callum whispered as he pulled the zipper of his sleeping bag all the way up to his chin, and tightened the hood until it completely encased his face.

'I know, right?' Adam whispered back, shivering slightly. 'It's like everyone gets home from school and work and then nobody leaves the house! I haven't heard a single car go past all night!'

'Me neither! The only thing I heard was this, like, kind of ... *crying* noise.'

'I know! I kept hearing it too! For *hours*! It sounded like everyone in the neighbourhood was crying at one point or another!'

It was very early morning and the brothers had been lying awake for hours, using their Cuddle Gnomes as very uncomfortable pillows and reading the magazine article about their dad over and over again, until they knew all of it off by heart – *Harry Beales was born and raised in Derry, has a bachelor's degree in physics, a PhD in information technology, never married, has no children, has worked at Stephington Industries for almost twenty years* ... And once they had exhausted all the information in the magazine, they spent the rest of the night chattering away to each other, having far too much to talk about to ever get any sleep.

By the time the sun came up, they were so tired, and so over-talked, that the words were almost coming out by themselves.

'And I can't believe Dad is actually *here*!' said Callum.

'I know, right?' yawned Adam.

'And ... but ... he's actually *here*, Adam!'

'I know!'

'And I can't believe it!'

'I *know*, Callum!'

'No, I mean, I *actually* can't believe it. It's just like when he died – I knew it was true, and that Mum wouldn't lie to us about something like that, but I couldn't make it make sense. I genuinely couldn't believe that it was real. Dad couldn't be dead because ... because he was our *dad*. He was always there, always in the kitchen when we woke up, always on the sofa in the evening, always driving the car when we went on holiday ... and then ... all of a sudden ... he ... wasn't. And it's the same now.

He's been gone for so long. And it feels like I've spent my whole life wishing he could come back, and it just doesn't feel like it can be *real*. I literally can't believe it.'

'Yeah, me too, I suppose,' said Adam, staring up at the ceiling of the shed. 'I don't think it will feel real until we actually see him.'

'And I can't believe we have to wait until we've *booked a meeting with him*! He's right here! Alive! In the same universe as us! In the same town as us! And we're just lying here, in a shed! And I could be hugging him, *right now*!'

'I know, right?'

'None of this is making sense to my brain, Adam. The whole thing is just, like …'

Callum mimed an explosion around his head. It had stopped making sense to Adam's brain *hours* ago, so much so that he was barely able to say more than the same three words over and over again …

'I know, right?' agreed Adam. 'It all kind of feels …'

Adam had been about to say 'too good to be true', about to say – *Things this good never happen to me! Things never go this right. Something bad always happens. I feel like I'm just waiting for something horrible to ruin it, to get in our way! To stop us from meeting Dad! To stop us from getting home!* But Adam didn't say any of that, deciding it would be best not to spread his doubt on to Callum, to keep it to himself. In fact, he was going to go one step further – not only would he not *talk* about it, he wasn't even going to *think* about it. There were just far too many emotions for Adam to handle, and every time he thought about it, it made him want to scream in fear, laugh with excitement, sob with heartbreak, so Adam shut his thoughts away, and let Callum's non-stop chatter numb his brain.

'And …' continued Callum, 'I can't believe Ethan is making us sleep in his *shed*! Hiding us away from his parents like we're a pair of escaped convicts!'

'*Sucks,* right?'

'And what about alti-Bruce? I can't believe what a nice guy he is!'

'I *know,* right? I still don't feel like I can trust him though. If there's even one per cent of *our* Bruce in

112

him, then he's probably just waiting for the perfect moment to double-cross us and find some way to gain from our pain.'

'And I can't believe the Popularis memory stick was addressed to Dad, at the same building where he works in the altiverse, and he's one of the top tech people in the world. It just seems like there's some kind of link between Dad and Popularis, don't you think?'

Adam's heart stopped beating entirely, then dropped into his stomach, where it hid and waited for the coast to be clear.

This is it. I'm finally going to have to tell him. I've avoided it long enough. I can't hide it any longer!

'Ah …'

Adam chewed his lip.

'Well, about that …'

His eyes searched the floor of the shed, the walls, the ceiling, *anywhere* but at Callum.

'You see, there's something I haven't told you about Popularis.'

Adam needed to swallow, and there was nothing he could do to stop it from becoming a huge GULP.

'It's not a big thing!' Adam insisted, leaning back on one elbow and doing his best to look relaxed and nonchalant. 'No big deal! Just a tiny detail that I never got around to mentioning, but ... well ... how do I put this? ... You see ... Dad invented Popularis and there's a little bit of him in there with the coding that sometimes makes it feel like Dad is talking to you from inside Popularis. That's all. So what are you going to order for breakfast tomorrow?'

'Whoa. Adam! What the ... Are you being *serious* right now? *Dad* invented Popularis, and you never told me?'

'But no one told me either,' Adam reasoned. 'It was one of those things where—'

'I've spent so much time wishing I could remember Dad as clearly as you do, and there was a bit of him inside Popularis the whole time?!'

'In my defence, you are always saying that you're old enough to figure things out for yourself, so I didn't think you'd want me to ruin the—'

'I *could* have figured it out for myself if you hadn't forced me never to use Popularis!' Callum wasn't whispering any more. He was properly shouting.

'Shhh!' pleaded Adam. 'Ethan's parents!'

'I don't care!' Callum yelled. 'You never told me, Adam! Why would you do that? If you thought there was a bit of Dad in there? How could you ignore him like that? How could you make *me* ignore him?!'

The guilt was threatening to eat Adam alive. But fighting back, battling against the guilt, was an entire battalion of anger. Adam had been *protecting* Callum. That's why he hadn't told him!

'I did it for the same reason I don't let you go down to the bowling alley and spend all your birthday money in the arcade – because even though it feels like it's going to be fun, it never goes your way, you never win loads of tickets back, you never get a decent prize, and you never leave feeling happier than when you went in. You always feel rubbish! And I didn't want anything else to go wrong for you. I didn't want you to feel rubbish. Not about Dad. That's why I told you to stay away from it. But you *didn't* ignore him, did you? You did mess with it! And now …'

'And now you're blaming it all on me again! Just

like you always do! Even when I didn't do anything wrong and *you did!* Because you never listen to me, Adam! NEVER! About ANYTHING! Like the millions of times I told you I didn't use Popularis on our B-Boys channel, but you never believed me!'

Callum's yells had become whimpers and whines. 'You *never* believe me, Adam. But I *didn't* use Popularis on our channel. I tried to tell you what I used it for, but you didn't want to listen to that either. I used it ... I used it to ... I used it to try to get to know Dad better. I wanted to know him like *you* knew him, when you used to go on days out together, for walks in the woods, camping weekends, trips to every theme park you could think of ... All the things I was too young to join in with. And now ... I think Popularis listened to me, even if you didn't. Because Popularis is giving me what I asked for!'

Callum's whimpers and whines had become grins and glee. 'Maybe this whole thing was Popularis's plan! My chance to get to know Dad! Maybe this is my wish coming true!'

Adam's army of anger had lost the battle. Guilt

reigned supreme. Guilt that he had never trusted Callum. Guilt that he had never listened to him. And guilt that Callum was going to end up more hurt and disappointed than ever.

There's no way that Popularis is doing this to grant Callum's wish, Adam thought. *First of all, Popularis does not grant wishes, he helps* solve problems, *usually in the most complicated and unhelpful way possible. And secondly, our dad in this altiverse isn't actually our dad. He's another* version *of our dad. A version who never had kids. A version who has no idea who we are! A* stranger. *But what do I do now? Do I tell Callum this, and break his heart again, or do I say nothing, and lose his trust even more for keeping more secrets from him?*

Callum's wide, hopeful eyes bored into Adam's, waiting for a response, waiting for some kind of confirmation that something *good* was happening to them, rather than something bad. And Adam didn't have the heart to crush that hope. Not yet. So Adam forced a smile.

'You know what, Cal? Maybe you're right. Maybe this whole thing *is* Popularis granting your wish.'

And then the shed door burst open, and there was

Ethan, standing in the open doorway with his hands on his hips. 'Remind me to explain to you what the word "quiet" means in our altiverse, because it seems to mean the exact *opposite* where you come from!'

Adam and Callum both grimaced in apology.

'The good news is that both my parents have left for work already. Oh, and breakfast is here! And, even better news, Bruce did it! He got you an interview! With your dead dad! Who's not dead. That was weird, wasn't it? I should have probably said that differently. Without using the word "dead". But I didn't. Anyway, your interview is at ten a.m.! In two hours! So you better come get some breakfast, brush your teeth, have a cry, then get your disguises on! Our mission is a *GO!*'

The excitement of the day ahead was just enough to distract Adam and Callum from Ethan's strange 'have a cry' suggestion, and more than enough to make up for the fact that neither Adam nor Callum had slept a wink all night.

'Do you have bacon sandwiches in your universe?' Bruce asked through a mouthful of breakfast as, standing barefoot in the dew-covered grass of

Ethan's back garden, he helped Adam get his hat on.

'We totally do,' replied Callum from inside the shed, where he was still getting into his outfit. 'But our ketchup isn't brown and garlicky. It's red.'

'Red?' gasped Bruce, almost choking on his sandwich. 'Mushrooms are *red* in your universe?'

Callum couldn't spit his food out fast enough.

'This ketchup is made of MUSHROOMS?!!?'

'What's *your* ketchup made of?' asked Ethan.

'Tomatoes, obviously!'

'Eeeuuurghhhh! *Tomatoes?*' squealed Bruce. 'That's *disgusting*! No one likes tomatoes!'

'That's a good point,' agreed Adam. 'We *hate* tomatoes!'

'Nobody likes mushrooms either, though!' Callum retorted.

'He's not wrong,' said Ethan. 'Why are both our ketchups made of stuff we hate? That's weird.'

'No,' said Adam. '*Weird* is me in this outfit.'

'Adam, it looks great!' Ethan assured him.

'Well, it *smells* weird.'

'But it looks great.'

'And it *feels* weird.'

'But it looks ... Adam, are you ever going to stop complaining?'

'Ethan, I am standing here in your grandma's best Sunday dress, which is two sizes too small, wearing your mum's most un-sensible shoes, with a ponytail made of doll's hair glued into the back of this baseball cap. I have never been more uncomfortable in my life! Of course I'm not going to stop complaining!'

'Well, I bet you any money your outfit is better than mine,' moaned Callum from inside the shed.

'I thought we agreed you were going to be a scientist?'

'Change of plan,' explained Ethan. 'Turns out Callum's quite a messy eater. He got fish all over his costume yesterday.'

'So?' asked Adam, wondering why that was such a huge problem.

'Well, my new kitten got hold of it. Turns out *she's* quite a messy eater too.' Ethan held up a coat hanger that had a few shreds of fabric dangling from it. 'That's all that's left of it. And since he can't exactly walk back in there looking like the same kid who ran rampage with a toilet brush yesterday, we had to find a last-minute replacement. You ready, Callum?'

The shed door slowly swung open, and out stepped Callum to reveal his disguise in all its glory.

It took Adam a few seconds to take in exactly what he was seeing. A few seconds to double-check that he wasn't dreaming it. A few seconds to start howling with uncontrollable laughter.

'You dressed him as a GIANT BANANA!'

'It was the only thing we had in his size,' said Ethan, with a shrug.

'Adam!' snapped Bruce sternly. 'Stop rolling on the ground! You'll ruin your dress!'

But Adam couldn't help it. Rolling on the ground, laughing, was the only sensible response!

'Cal, pass me your camera, I have to get a photo of this!'

'Are you kidding me?' snapped Callum. 'It's on nineteen per cent! And it's probably the only screen in this entire universe! If the battery runs down, it won't matter if we get Popularis up and running again, because we won't have anything to talk to him on!'

Adam instantly stopped laughing.

'Whoa. I never even thought about that. Cal,

that's the most sensible thing you've ever said in your life. New rule – from now on, keep your phone turned off until we need it.'

Adam got up off the grass, the picture of seriousness, except ...

'Adam?' said Callum. 'You've got a dandelion stuck in your knickers.'

The dandelion definitely did not help with Adam's comfort issues. And his discomfort didn't end there. When they hopped on the bus to Stephington Industrial Estate, Adam got to experience the most uncomfortable journey of his life.

'What? How ... W-where are the *seats*?' Callum stammered as they made their way down the gangway. 'I don't get it!'

'I have no idea,' Adam mumbled in confusion.

From the outside, it looked just like an ordinary bus. But on the inside it did not look like a bus at all. Instead of being lined with rows of seats down either side of the gangway, this bus was lined with *cubicles*. Like toilet cubicles, but without toilets in them. Without doors. Without *anything* in them.

Just one person, standing in each cubicle, holding on to a handle, and staring at either a single poster on the wall or at the world outside. And of course, in their nervous fluster, Adam and Callum managed to get it completely wrong …

'What are we supposed to do?' Callum whispered urgently as the bus began moving. 'The bus driver's giving me dodgy looks! Let's ask Ethan!'

But Ethan and Bruce had already disappeared into their own cubicles, further down the bus.

'Just get inside one of the things!' Adam hissed as he leaped into the nearest empty cubicle, closely followed by Callum.

'But there's only one handle!' Callum complained as the lurching bus tossed him around the cubicle like a banana in a bungee jumper's backpack.

'We don't both fit in here!' Adam growled. 'It's too small! I can't even – *ouch*! My toes!'

'Sorry!' whispered Callum. 'But I'm not going back out there now! Did you see the way everyone was staring at me? It was weird, Adam. *Weird*. It's like they *know* we don't belong here!'

'Yeah,' Adam whispered back. 'It could be that,

or it could be that you're dressed as a giant banan—
Ouch! Watch your elbows!'

'*Shhh!* You're making too much noise! Listen to that …' Callum paused and let the silence of the bus take over. 'No one else is *talking*. No one else is making any noise at all!'

Callum was right. Even stranger than the cubicles-instead-of-seats thing was that not a single person was making the slightest bit of noise.

'OK, this just keeps getting weirder and weirder,' groaned Adam. 'VZs, not going in other people's houses, no *socialising on buses* … I'm beginning to think that the reason they haven't invented phones in this altiverse is because they don't *want* to invent phones! No one wants to talk to each other here! It's almost as if – *ouch!* The end of your banana is poking me in the – *OUCH!*'

If Callum thought he was getting funny looks getting *on* the bus, it was nothing compared to the looks they got getting *off* it – eye rolls, angry shakes of the head, disapproving glares …

'Why didn't you explain how the buses work?' Callum snapped at Ethan as they hurried off the bus.

'How was I supposed to know your buses aren't the same as ours?' Ethan retorted defensively.

'Think about it, guys, it's not like we can explain *everything* in the altiverse, just in case some of it happens to be slightly different to yours,' Bruce calmly added.

'We'd be here all day!' said Ethan. 'And, in case you didn't notice, we're on a bit of a tight schedu—'

'These are the ones,' growled the bus driver, who, to Adam's horror, had got off the bus and led a police officer over to them! 'These two, here.'

The grey-haired police officer gave Adam a simmering glare over the top of her gold-rimmed spectacles as the driver walked away.

'I would expect someone of your age to set a better example for her child,' admonished the police officer.

'Oh! I ... yes!' gasped Adam, making a valiant yet terrible attempt to sound like a lady. 'I'm sorry, your highness ... I mean *excellency* ... I mean ... *officer*. We got a little confused and ... a little turned around, and ... we ... erm ... we're not from round here.'

'Hmmmm, yes, I can see that,' said the police officer, eyeing Callum's banana outfit with interest. 'That's why I'm going to let you off.'

Adam breathed an audible sigh of relief.

'But from now on, please be aware that riding two to a compartment and conversing on public transport are not permitted and are punishable with a fixed penalty.'

'Thank you, officer. We won't do it again!' Adam gratefully assured her.

'I believe you won't. Have a good day.'

And to Adam's huge relief, the police officer began to walk away. Then, to Adam's utter horror, she turned back when Callum piped up.

'How would we know the rules if no one is allowed to talk to us and tell us about them?' Callum asked.

The police officer stared at him, completely stunned.

'I mean, how do you share information … or knowledge … or feelings if you don't talk to each other?'

Adam could not believe what Callum was doing!

He didn't know whether to laugh or cry or run away as fast as possible!

He's going to get us arrested, and we'll miss our appointment with Dad! Adam screamed inside his head. *I KNEW this was too good to be true!*

But, to Adam's surprise, instead of slapping them both in handcuffs, the police officer actually *smiled*. It was a puzzled, confused smile, but it was still a smile.

'What a peculiar word you used – *share* – as if passing information to one another is a *kind* thing to do? We usually say that we *spread* information, like how one person might spread germs to another. Too much information will clog up the brain. But yes, you make a good point, we do need to put more signs up to remind people.'

'Well, can I *share* a piece of information with you? It was pretty cool of you to tell us the rules and not arrest us. You're OK, you know,' Callum said.

The look of puzzlement on the police officer's face got way bigger, but so did her smile.

'Well, thank you, I suppose. And you're welcome.'

'Thank-you-goodbye!' Adam chirped as he began dragging Callum away before he could say anything else.

But Callum wasn't going anywhere. He broke free from Adam and walked right up to the police officer.

'And maybe, if you talk to someone about what's making you sad, you might start to feel better about it,' he said softly.

Her eyes widened and her mouth dropped open.

'H-how did you know I'm sad?' she whispered, her eyes turning pink and moist.

'Your tissue, poking out of your pocket. It's covered in mascara, just like Mum's when we've been to visit Dad's grave.'

'Oh, I ...' The police officer looked to Adam. 'I'm so sorry for your loss. It must be so difficult for you, with the little one.'

'*Two* little ones,' Adam pointed out. 'I have another. Adam. He's the smart one.'

'Oh, I find it hard to believe anyone could be smarter than this little banana!' laughed the police officer, a tear escaping her eye, which she quickly mopped up with her tissue.

'You're right,' agreed Callum. 'Adam's a bit of an idiot, really. And he smells.'

The police lady laughed even more as she turned back to Adam.

'Well, you're doing a wonderful job to raise such a lovely child ... *children*.'

'Thank you,' said Adam, wishing his mum had heard that, and, still thinking of his mum, he added, 'I suppose I am, really.'

It was no longer just Adam and Callum getting odd looks from passers-by – the police officer was also getting some very disapproving glances.

'Oh dear,' she whispered conspiratorially, 'a police officer laughing, crying *and* talking in public! I best be on my way before I get *myself* in trouble, but it was lovely to meet you both.'

'Don't forget,' Callum whispered back, 'a problem shared is a problem halved. That's what Mum always says.'

'Well, we usually say, "Keep your worries locked

inside, and your problems learn to run and hide," but I'll think about your one,' said the police officer as she carried on walking, smiling and crying more than ever.

'Are you done?' snapped Ethan. 'While you're stood out here convincing a police officer to *break the law*, you're missing your meeting! It started five minutes ago!'

8

Banana Split

By the time they reached Stephington Industries they were *ten* minutes late. And by the time they'd waited in line at the front desk, then waited for the receptionist to finish making notes in his big black book, they were *fifteen* minutes late.

Adam's heart sank when the receptionist told them, 'I'm afraid you're too late. Mr Beales is in another meeting now. But you're welcome to take a seat, and I can see if he can squeeze you in afterwards?'

So all four of them shuffled to the seating area, up on the concourse, directly beneath the part of the roof which, the previous morning, back in their universe, had had a huge tree poking through it.

'OK, so, obviously, Callum, we couldn't set up a business meeting for a kid in a banana suit,' said Ethan. 'So, on the very slim chance that your dad *will* make another meeting for you, you'll just have to wait out here while Adam does the—'

'WHAT?' Callum blurted in outrage, causing everyone else in the waiting area to jump out of their seats. 'Are you kidding me? It's my *dad*! I want to see him too! I *have to*!'

'Callum, relax!' whispered Adam. '*If* he'll see me, I'll make up some story about you being a huge fan of his or something, and I'll see if I can get you in at the end of the meeting, OK?'

'No, you *will* get me in at the end of the meeting,' Callum insisted.

'Yes, fine, I *will* get you in at the end of the meeting. I promise. I know it's difficult, and I know it's not fair, but you *have* to wait until I call you in, OK? I'm supposed to be a professional business-woman, and professional businesswomen do not take their kids along to meetings, OK?'

'Fine,' Callum huffed as he crossed his arms and

pushed himself into the back of his chair as hard as he could.

Office People began appearing from doorways, calling Waiting People in for meetings, like doctors calling in patients from a waiting room, and Adam instantly began sweating with anxiety.

What if we messed up by being late? What if he won't see me?

And then his heart began to pound as he thought of an even greater anxiety –

What if he WILL see me? What do I say? It's DAD!

Just like all his other worries, he tried not to think about it. He sat up straight. Adjusted his ponytail. Popped a mint in his mouth. Then froze.

'Wait. Bruce, what name did you book my meeting under? How will I know when they call me? Or have they *already* called me?'

Just then, a secretary stepped into the waiting area and called the next person.

'Professor Marvel-Universe?'

'You're up!' said Bruce.

Adam almost choked on his mint, sending it

flying from his mouth and into the back of a random man's head.

'*Professor Marvel-Universe?!*' Adam spluttered.

'What?' said Bruce defensively. 'That's not your surname? But it was written all over your pyjamas!'

'Brilliant!' chuckled Callum as Adam got to his feet and followed the secretary towards an office. 'Good luck, Mum! I'm *Grooting* for you!'

Adam entered the office and immediately ground to a halt. There, sat on the other side of a big desk, was his *dad*. His real live dad! In the flesh! Looking at Adam with the same eyes that Adam used to lovingly gaze into as a child. And resting on the desk were the same arms that used to give Adam such tight bedtime cuddles. Beneath the desk were his legs that used to dance ridiculously to

Stevie Wonder in the kitchen. There were his ears that two-year-old Adam used to use as handles whenever he'd get a shoulder ride in the park. His beard that Adam used to hide Lego figures in, pretending it was The Forest of Doom …

Adam had known it was going to be a big deal seeing his dad again, but he hadn't prepared himself for just how COLOSSALLY HUGE it was going to feel inside! In his heart. In his throat. In his tear ducts, which were threatening to spill over like Niagara Falls!

'Professor Marvel-Universe? Are you feeling OK?' asked the man behind the desk. Professor Harry Beales. *Dad.*

'Mmm-hmm!' Adam managed to grunt, his voice almost cracking into a full-on sob.

Adam had intended to apologise for being late, and to thank his dad for seeing him. No chance. He could barely form a single word.

'Are you *sure?*'

'I fine!' Adam squeaked. 'Hay fever!'

'Oh dear, yes, can I get you anything?'

'I fine!'

Adam still hadn't moved from the doorway, where he appeared to be glued to the spot.

'Please, take a seat.'

'OK!'

Adam's wobbly legs managed to slowly and shakily transport him across the room, tripping occasionally in the high heels, like a newborn foal learning to walk.

'I had no idea hay fever could have such an effect on someone's *legs*,' said Mr Beales sympathetically.

'Yes!' spluttered Adam, holding back the urge to dive across the desk and give his dad an almighty, tear-drenched hug. 'Very bad!'

Adam finally sat down, and tried to stop his bottom lip from trembling while he stared at the desk (he knew he'd never be able to keep it together if he looked his dad in the eyes).

'So,' said Mr Beales, clearly feeling a little awkward about Professor Marvel-Universe's peculiar behaviour, 'you've come to discuss a project of yours called the *InterNET,* is that right?'

'Mmm-hmm!'

'And … could you shed a little more light on this subject?'

'Mmm-hmm!'

'Oh good. Err … *now?*'

'Mmm-hmm! Uh … Erm … Lots of wires. Cables. And information. Data. Travels through the cables. All over the world. Mmm-hmm!'

That was the best Adam could manage. He was blowing the whole meeting and he knew it! But he couldn't help it! The world's biggest sob-fest was building up inside him and threatening to explode at any minute!

Mr Beales was silent for an awkwardly long time. And when Adam finally braved a glance up at his face, he was surprised to see that his dad looked *amazed*.

'Oh. My. Word!' Harry gasped, grinning from ear to ear. 'This sounds like exactly the same idea I've been working on!'

Adam's heart leaped with excitement, and for a second he almost forgot to feel emotional.

So he IS inventing the internet! YES! We CAN get back home!

'Take a look!' exclaimed Harry, jumping to his feet and rushing over to an object in the corner of the room.

The chest-height object was shrouded in a large blanket, which Harry grabbed hold of, ready to whip it away for a big reveal.

'Allow me to introduce the *World … Wide … Web*!'

Harry snatched the blanket away to uncover a globe of planet Earth, and pinned all around the globe was a literal web of strings, resembling a global network, just like that of the early internet.

'Yes!' Adam blurted. 'The World Wide Web! Or WWW for short. Or actually for *long*. I mean, it's only three letters, but it takes a lot longer to say than the three whole words so … I sound like Ethan, don't I? But you don't know who Ethan is, so … Yes! The World Wide Web! The internet! You're doing it! You have no idea how relieved – I mean, *excited* I am!'

'I've never met anyone as excited by this as I am!' laughed Harry, feasting on Adam's enthusiasm. 'I've only known you a few minutes and already I feel as if we could be the best of friends!'

'Well … likewise!' Adam laughed. 'I already feel as if I've known you my whole life!'

Adam's heart was dancing with joy! It was happening! The meeting was happening! The internet was happening! Seeing his dad again was happening! And going back home would soon be happening too! He was wrong – it *wasn't* too good to be true!

'And you said something about making this work all around the world?' Harry almost squealed in excitement. 'That's exactly what we've been struggling with! We just can't make it reach that far! Wait – let me call my boss in! She has to meet you!'

Harry dashed from his office, and returned a minute later with his boss in tow.

Adam took one look at Harry's boss and his jaw hit the floor.

'Y-y-you're *Steph Kilter*! Your Bruce's mum! And ... you're the *boss* here? Why didn't anyone tell me?!'

'Well, my dear, I thought the name *Steph*ington Industries might have provided an adequate clue,' purred Mrs Kilter as she made herself comfortable in Harry's chair. 'So, Harry tells me you have an idea that could improve upon our already perfect designs for the InterNAL. Something about making this a *global* network, which I already know to be impossible.'

Adam said nothing. Just as his heart had begun to soar from how perfectly everything was falling into place, seeing Bruce's mum had sent it crashing back down. He could just about believe that alti-Bruce might not be as mean as home-Bruce, but he only had to take one look at alti-Steph Kilter, and the way she sneered at him, to see that she was every bit as evil as home-Steph. No, *eviler*! And Adam didn't want to tell her anything. Back in his universe, Stan and Steph Kilter were only ever interested in lying and cheating and stealing, and Adam had a feeling that this Steph was no different. But at the same time, seeing his dad's happy, eager face smiling at him so expectantly, he didn't want to let him down. He wanted to tell him everything he knew about how the internet worked!

'Well …' said Adam, biting his lip in deliberation. 'You see …'

Steph eyed him with a smirk of scepticism.

Harry shuffled to the edge of his seat, hanging on Adam's every word.

Adam made his mind up.

'OK, listen carefully, this is how it works …'

The office door burst open, and in charged a four-foot banana that launched itself at a very bemused Harry.

'DADDY! IT'S ME! I LOVE YOU!!!'

'CALLUM! NO!' Adam yelled.

'Goodness me!' howled Mrs Kilter, leaping away from the intruder.

'Adam said you won't know me, but you *do*! Look!'

Callum jumped on to his dad's lap, and wrapped a loving arm around his neck as he pulled his phone from his banana pocket, and began flicking through old family photos and videos that he kept in their own special album.

'Callum, the battery!' Adam pleaded. 'You'll run it down!'

'SECURITY!' Mrs Kilter wailed at the top of her voice.

But Adam noticed that her wailing came to an abrupt halt the second her greedy eyes caught sight of Callum's phone.

'That's us on my third birthday!' Callum hurriedly explained. 'That's us on our holiday to Cork! That's a video of us on Christmas morning!'

Harry stared at the screen, utterly dumbfounded.

Adam stared at Mrs Kilter with increasing distrust as she sidled towards Callum's phone, eyes wide and hands even wider.

'Callum, look out!'

Three security guards burst into the office. Steph lunged for Callum's phone. Adam dragged Callum away, narrowly escaping the clutches of the security guards as he ran for the door.

'STOP THEM!!!!' barked Mrs Kilter.

A security guard got a hold of Adam's ponytail, but it came away in his hand.

'Arghh!!' screamed Adam. 'You BRUTE!'

'What are you doing, Adam?!' wailed Callum, as they raced across the concourse and down the stairs. 'What's going on?!'

'Our situation just got a whole lot worse!' yelled Adam, as they raced from the building. '*That's* what's going on!'

9

The Unexpected VZtor

After running away from Stephington Lane, followed by a long period of hiding in a park, followed by an achingly long walk back from the city centre, Adam and Callum finally trudged into Ethan's back garden later that same day. Adam's partially destroyed ponytailed cap was on sideways, Callum's banana suit was soaked in sweat, and both of them looked as if they had just completed *Total Wipeout* five times in a row.

'Where did you two disappear to?' asked Ethan, frantic with worry as he rushed out of his house to meet them. 'I didn't know what had happened to you! There were security guys all over the place! People were screaming! I thought you'd been arrested. And then Bruce's mum comes out, all flustered and furious, and she drags Bruce away, shouting stuff like, "*Who were those two people you came in with?! Where are they? What were you doing with them?*" And then I was all by myself, and I didn't know what to do, so I just sat there and waited for, like, two hours! What *happened*?'

'Two things happened,' groaned Adam as he collapsed on to his back in front of Ethan's shed. 'First of all, Callum ruined everything. Second of all, Bruce's mum turned into a psychopath. I think that sums everything up.'

'Oh,' said Ethan, his motor-mouth struggling to get into gear, 'so, er ... the meeting wasn't a success then?'

'Not unless, in this altiverse, "success" means "a massive barrel of poo", no.'

'Well, I'm afraid I've got some more bad news for you,' Ethan said with a grimace. 'My parents will be back from work in a few minutes, so, like, you'll have to hide in the shed again. Sorry!'

'Don't worry about it, Ethan. It's not a problem,' Adam sighed as he crawled back into the shed. 'Just as long as I'm not sharing that shed with anyone dressed as a banana who just literally destroyed my entire universe.'

'I said I'm sorry a *million* times,' muttered Callum as he followed Adam into the shed.

'A million sorrys? Great! Just enough sorrys for us to build a computer with! Oh no, wait, you can't build a computer from sorrys, can you? That's what we needed alti-Dad for. I remember now. Shame.'

'I'll, erm, leave you to it,' said Ethan as he slowly began to close the shed door behind them. 'I'll order you some dinner and bring it out when it gets here.'

The door was almost shut when Adam called back to him.

'Ethan? Why didn't Bruce tell me that his mum owns Stephington Industries? Why didn't *you* tell me?'

'Well … Do you guys really talk about personal stuff in your universe? Only … it's kind of weird. Family stuff is *personal*. No one talks about things like that here.'

'OK, it's just that … I don't know. It would have

been good to know, that's all. Only … back in our universe, Bruce's whole family are a bit … you know, *evil*. And today, at the office, Bruce's mum totally went for Callum's phone.'

'OK, well, I feel kind of weird talking about someone else's family, Adam,' Ethan admitted. 'Sorry.'

And Ethan shut the door with a *clunk*.

The brothers listened as Ethan's footsteps walked back across the garden, and into his house, then Callum quickly pounced on the opportunity to steer the subject away from himself.

'Adam! Another thing about Bruce …' he whispered, 'Ethan said that Bruce's mum was asking him about us! But how did she know he was with us?'

'That's a good point,' said Adam. 'She *couldn't* have known, unless …'

'Unless Bruce had already told her about us,' said Callum.

'Which means Bruce isn't keeping our secret. And if we can't trust Bruce to keep our secret, then he'll tell her exactly where to find us. Where to find your *phone*. And before you know it …'

Both brothers almost leaped out of their skins as a *KNOCK-KNOCK-KNOCK* reverberated through the shed. They both froze. Both stared at each other in surprise. And both mouthed the same two words at each other – '*Steph Kilter!*'

The knock came again, and Adam finally replied with a whispered 'Hello?'

'Hi,' a barely-there voice on the other side of the shed replied. 'Is it OK if I come in?'

Adam tried desperately to put a face to the voice – was it Bruce's mum? Bruce's *dad*, even?

Bruce himself? But that's the thing about whispered voices – they all sound the same!

'Err … who is it?' said Adam, sitting up straight in his sleeping bag while trying and failing to free his head from the fully tightened hood.

The door opened, and neither Adam nor Callum could breathe as the visitor let themselves in.

'I hope you don't mind the intrusion, especially since this shed doesn't come equipped with a VZ, but our meeting came to such an abrupt halt earlier, I was wondering if we might carry it on here, in your, err, *shed*?'

Harry Beales looked expectantly at Callum, but Callum couldn't speak. So he turned to Adam just as he managed to free himself from the sleeping bag, causing Mr Beales to step back in surprise.

'Oh! I do apologise! I thought you were Professor Marvel-Universe!'

Adam touched his head – no cap! No ponytail! No disguise!

'No!' he blurted. 'I … We … It was a disguise. I *am* Professor Marvel-Universe! It's just …'

'Relax,' his dad laughed. 'I'm joking. I figured it

out by myself. Not that it wasn't a great disguise, but, just for future reference, most PhD graduates who wear lipstick usually just put it on their *lips*, rather than their lips and a bit on their chin, and some on their teeth and cheeks and ... I think you even managed to get some on your *nose*.'

'I told you you should have let me do it!' hissed Callum.

'Listen, about what happened before ... I ... wait ... how did you *find us*?' Adam puzzled.

'I used a special location-tracking device we've been developing at work,' explained Harry. 'We call it – "*Bruce*"!'

Bruce poked his head in through the shed door and gave a little wave.

'Hello!'

'You mentioned his name in our meeting, and, since I've known him his entire life, I guessed he was the man to go to,' Harry explained.

'The man that *everyone* goes to,' Adam muttered under his breath.

'You've known him his entire ... *what*?' said Callum, unable to get his head around this.

'He's my boss's son,' said Harry. 'I bought him his very first Cuddle Gnome!'

'But, like, what happened?' Adam asked Bruce. 'Ethan said your mum was pretty mad with you. Said she knew that you were the one who got us in.'

'Yeah,' Bruce sighed. 'Turns out, after the big misunderstanding, they checked the visitor book and saw that I was the one who signed you in, so I had a bit of explaining to do. Don't worry though! I didn't tell anyone anything. Just that you two are friends of mine who are really big fans of Harry's, and that you had some really cool ideas to share with him.'

'And, sorry, this is so confusing!' said Adam, shaking his head slightly as if this might dislodge the confusion. 'Da— *Harry*, you figured out we were imposters, and you still want to finish our meeting? How do you know my story wasn't as fake as my disguise?'

'Oh, easy!' declared Harry. 'I *did* think your story was fake! Well, not at first but … It was your *faces* that I believed.'

'Our *what?*'

'Well, *his* face, to be precise,' said Harry, looking back to Callum with a smile. 'Take a look ...'

Harry reached into his inside pocket and pulled out an old black-and-white photo of Callum on a trike.

'Whoa!' Adam gasped. 'How did you get this? And Callum, when did you ever own a bike like *that*?'

Callum was still speechless.

Harry was still smiling.

'That isn't Callum,' he explained. 'It's *me*, about thirty years ago! Seeing this little banana come running into my office was like going back in time and looking at *myself*. And then when he started calling me "Daddy" and showing me those moving pictures ... well, I knew something truly special was happening. That's why I came here, for you to fill me in on precisely what's going on.'

So that's exactly what they did. Bruce said his goodbyes, explaining that 'This feels a bit too personal for me to join in with,' leaving Adam and Callum to explain the whole story to their not-dead not-dad. They told him every last detail – about how they'd travelled from an alternate universe, about how, back there, he was their dad, about the internet, Popularis, the memory stick with the source code, computers, smartphones, and how they were now stuck there, with no way home ... And when they finished, the three of them sat there for five long, silent minutes until Harry finally spoke.

'Yeah, I thought that was what you'd say,' he said, nodding his head.

'*What?*' Adam and Callum both gasped at the same time.

'Well, maybe not the bit about "computers" – you have to admit, that bit does sound a bit far-fetched. But when I saw your face, Callum, and you took out that futuristic device of yours, with moving photos, with *me* in them ... well, there weren't many other explanations.'

'You even guessed about *Popularis*?' Adam asked disbelievingly.

'I've been dreaming about inventing something like that all my life,' said Harry with a shrug. 'Stands to reason that I'd succeed in one reality or another!'

'And you don't find any of this whole "in-turdy-mentioning travel" thing difficult to believe?' asked Callum.

Harry gave a long, sorrowful sigh.

'I'm afraid the only difficulty about this whole thing is the "getting you back home" part.'

'I was afraid you'd say that,' groaned Adam. 'It's impossible, right?'

'It *was* impossible *two days ago*, but now you two have actually *done it*, and that proves that it *is* possible. And if it was possible once, then it's certainly possible twice.'

'So ... what do we do?' asked Callum.

'Simple,' said Harry, rubbing his hands together with eager excitement. 'We get to work! We *invent* what we need, and then we get you two home!'

He gave Adam a high five, one of those ones that almost turns into a handshake, and Adam gave a whoop of excitement. Callum got the next high five. But Callum didn't whoop with excitement. He held on tight to his dad's hand as though he never wanted to let go.

10

His Tree Repeating Itself

The next morning couldn't have come quick enough. After Harry left, Adam and Callum both fell asleep happy, friends once again. And they were up at the crack of dawn, eager to meet up with their alti-dad and to get started on finding a way to get back home.

The day began with three pieces of paper – the first was a note they left for Ethan inside the shed, explaining where they had gone, the second was Harry's home address that he had written down for them, and the third was a family ticket he had given them, so that they could catch a bus there (which they decided they would do *properly* this time, without almost getting arrested!).

'What do you think his house is like?' wondered Callum, as they stepped off the bus and began walking towards Charcoal Street.

'He's one of the top tech brains in the world, Cal. He probably lives in a luxurious mansion, with glass walls and fancy furniture,' Adam guessed.

But when they reached Harry's address, the building they arrived at was … well, it was whatever the *opposite* of a 'luxurious mansion' is!

'Are you sure this is the right place?' asked Callum, snatching the address from Adam's hand and double-checking the street name and door number.

'It doesn't seem right, right?' said Adam as he wandered up and down the dingy little side alley, searching for any door that didn't resemble a ware-house fire exit.

'This *is* number two-hundred and twenty-two Charcoal Street, but … it *can't* be the right place, can it?' said Callum, staring up at the dirty grey metal door that was nestled between two huge wheelie bins. 'It doesn't even have a *handle*.'

'Or a letter box, or a doorbell, or one of those

VZ things. It doesn't even have a proper house number …' added Adam.

In fact, the only clue that this *was* a door and not just a slab of metal set into a wall was that it had a keyhole, and a small '222' written on it in black marker pen.

'And what's *that* thing?' puzzled Callum, pointing up to a strange trumpet-like contraption that hung above the door, with a short rope dangling from the middle of it. 'Is it supposed to be … a *bell*?'

Adam reached up, gave the rope a little jiggle and a metal ball at the top of the rope collided with the sides of the trumpet with an ugly CLANG-A-LANG-A-LANG!!

'Ooh!' came a tinny voice, seemingly from nowhere. 'Is that you?'

'Erm …' said Adam, looking for some kind of speaker or microphone to talk into. 'Yes, I am me. Could *anyone* answer "no" to that question?'

'Good point, Adam!' replied the voice. 'Let me try that again – is that you, Adam?'

'Err … yes. Is that you, Da— *Harry*?'

'The one and only! Or, well, actually, *not* the one and only, as we have recently discovered.'

'Adam,' Callum whispered. 'I think the voice is coming from the *trumpet*.'

'Absolutely right, Callum!' Harry's tinny voice confirmed. 'I call it the ExterNAL – a sort of prototype for the InterNAL, in a way.'

'That's great,' muttered Adam while wishing he had something warmer to wear than just his pyjamas. 'Do you think we could come in?'

'Ooh! Yes! Of course! Step inside.'

There was a soft *click* sound of a door unlocking, but the big grey door didn't budge. Adam tried to get his fingers around the edge to prise it open, but it was no use.

'Can you try that again?' Adam called up to the hanging trumpet. 'The door's still locked.'

'Ooh! No, not the *door*. The *bin*!' the tinny voice replied.

Adam turned to the wheelie bin to his right and was amazed to see that the entire side of it had swung open, revealing a wood-panelled interior, with a small, velvet-covered bench against the back wall and thick, soft carpet on the floor, and a bright blue Cuddle Gnome nestled in one corner.

'Please, step inside! Take a seat!' Harry's voice instructed.

'OK, so we're getting into a bin with seats in,' Adam muttered to himself as he cautiously ducked into the plastic box. 'Of course we are. Why go in through a door when we can get into a bin instead? Makes perfect sense!'

The door began to close before they'd even sat down, and the second they were in their seats the bin lurched into motion.

'WHOA!' Adam and Callum both exclaimed at once, clutching on to the walls in alarm.

'Are we *moving*?' asked Callum.

'Uh-huh!' Adam confirmed shakily. 'And I think we're going *up*!'

The bin shuddered and shook as it slowly edged up the outside of the building, like some bizarre altiverse-lift, draining the colour from the brothers' faces with every rattle and squeak. Finally it came to a stop, and the door automatically swung open. Adam glimpsed a bird's-eye view of Derry's

skyline as he and Callum stepped out on to an iron fire escape balcony, three storeys high, and in through another metal doorway that a cheerful Harry Beales was holding open for them.

'Come in! Come in!' he cheered as he ushered the brothers into his home. 'Did you enjoy the ride up? My own design! All done with magnets!'

'*Magnets*? Great,' Adam grunted as he swallowed back the urge to be sick. 'Loved it. The most comfortable bin I've ever been in.'

'Ever *bin* in,' chuckled Callum as he gleefully

hopped from the balcony, into Harry's apartment, then straight into Adam's back.

'What did you stop walking for?' Callum complained, rubbing his sore nose, which had just collided with Adam's shoulder blade.

'Whooooaaaaa!' said Adam, gazing all around at the interior of Harry's home. 'Amazing!'

Far from being a luxury mansion with glass walls and fancy furniture, Harry's home, or lab, or *lair*, was filled, wall-to-wall, floor-to-ceiling, with weird and wonderful homemade gadgets and gizmos (and Cuddle Gnomes): there were paper aeroplanes that travelled along wires, propelled by magnets as they shot in and out of an open window, seemingly sending and delivering messages (and there was a Cuddle Gnome on the window ledge); there were telescope-like objects at every window, with the front ends pointing down to a different part of Derry, and the back ends sending daylight-powered projections of those images directly on to Harry's walls – one image of the traffic on Foyle Bridge, another image of the city skyline, even a close-up image of a magpie's nest in a nearby tree – like some sort of wire-free, screenless CCTV cameras (and there was a Cuddle Gnome sat on a shelf); and over in one corner of the room was a square sheet of steel that seemed to be floating two feet off the ground, entirely of its own accord. (And there was a Cuddle Gnome sat on top of it.) Everywhere Adam looked, there was some kind of out-of-this-world contraption, far too many to take in, far too amazing to comprehend. (Oh, and quite a lot of Cuddle Gnomes.)

'This …' began Callum.

'Is …' continued Adam.

'*Awesome!*' they concluded as one.

'*Really?*' said Harry, somehow sounding amazed and surprised and bashful and proud all at once. 'Thank you!'

'But what's with all the Cuddle Gnomes? Do you have kids?' asked Adam, wondering if there *were* altiverse versions of himself and Callum after all.

Harry let out a huge belly laugh. 'Do I look like the kind of person to get married and have kids?'

'Well …' Adam gestured to Callum and himself.

'We wouldn't exist if you weren't the kind of person to have kids!'

'Good point. No, Adam, no kids. Not in this universe, at least. The Cuddle Gnomes are all mine. Please don't tell me they're just for children in your universe? How sad. *Everyone* has a dozen or so Cuddle Gnomes because ... well, *everyone needs cuddles* from time to time!'

'Ahhhh, I see!' said Adam, finally piecing together what Cuddle Gnomes were all about – they weren't like teddy bears for kids to play with and snuggle up to in bed, they were to make up for the fact that nobody in the altiverse was allowed to spend proper time together, or talk in public, or discuss personal information. Everyone in the altiverse was *lonely* and needed to cuddle something! Even if that 'something' was a strange little gnome with not-very-comforting-actually spring-loaded arms. 'I guess that's kind of cool.'

'Not as cool as all of these gadgets!' Callum quickly corrected him, his voice blaring through the apartment as he messed around with some kind of altiverse megaphone made from tin cups. 'Whoa! Way too loud. I'll put that down. Sorry. It's just, this is some of the coolest stuff I've ever seen in my life!'

'But … *how*?' Harry seemed genuinely baffled. 'Your universe sounds so much more scientifically advanced than ours!'

'Well, yeah,' Adam conceded, 'but at the same time, *no*. I mean, we do have smartphones and space rockets and the *internet,* but … your things are just so awesome! And it looks like almost *everything* is powered by *magnets*! How are you not, like, the richest man in the world? These inventions are *amazing*.'

'Hmm, that's nice of you to say, but, until the InterNAL, my only successful invention was the Order Box – you know, that device with the buttons that people use to order their meals.'

'*What?!*' gasped Callum, who was now standing on top of the floating piece of metal and bouncing up and down on it like it was a trampoline. 'But you've made so much spectacular stuff! How have you only had one hit? I thought you were, like, a tech *wizard*! One of the biggest tech brains in the world!'

'I *am* one of the biggest tech brains in the world. Trouble is, no one really *wants* tech here. I'm sure that in your universe everyone loves technology, but being the top tech brain in *this* universe is a bit like being the top *worm* guy, or the top *sewage* guy – you might be the best at what you do, but it doesn't make what you do any more popular! But that's where Stephington Industries are making a differ-ence – they're turning *bad* ideas into popular ones! Into inventions that actually assist in our day-to-day lives! You see, most of my ideas are useless ones, to do with communication – sending messages via mag-planes, dropping in on each other with the camera telescopia, building floating bridges so we can get from one place to another more easily, that sort of stuff.'

'And …?' Adam urged him. 'What's the problem with that? They're brilliant ideas!'

'Adam, I don't know how things work in your universe, but in ours, people don't want to visit, or drop in, or send messages to each other. We live in a NAL society. My ideas are literally some of the worst inventions since the *bus*, and the guy who

invented buses got *thrown in jail*, until the Kilters came up with the idea of adding cubicles!'

'This is making my head spin! People *don't* like tech?' said Adam indignantly. 'And what even is this NAL thing everyone keeps talking about?'

'Well, quite simply, NAL stands for Nice and Lonely. It's how we live here. We keep ourselves to ourselves, and we don't burden each other with our problems or invade anyone's personal space. It just isn't done.'

'Yeah, we kind of got that,' said Callum, getting out of breath from all the bouncing. 'In our world we don't make our guests sleep in the *shed*.'

'And in our world there's no such word as "guest", but I think I can figure out what it means,' said Harry.

'But you've brought us *here*. Isn't this your personal space? Isn't this breaking the rules or something?' asked Adam.

'*Totally* breaking the rules! But that's the beauty of having a floating bin outside your house – no one knows who or what is inside it!' Harry chuckled. 'Incidentally, that's another one of my more useless ideas that Steph Kilter has adapted to work on a day-to-day level, shrinking it down and turning it into a lunch lift, so people can have their meals delivered directly to their offices without actually having to *see* the delivery person! That's going to be next year's big release, after we've finished rolling out the InterNAL.'

'So, what's so special about this InterNAL thing?' asked Callum. 'How come everyone likes *that* invention?'

'Well, they like it because it's a communication device that lets people be even *lonelier*,' explained Harry.

'That actually makes no sense at all,' Adam informed him. 'How can communicating with people make you lonely? It's not even possible.'

'I'll show you!'

Harry walked over to a desk next to a window where a row of three small metal cups sat, upside down, with pieces of string trailing from them that went up and out through three circular holes in the wall. Harry picked up the first cup, held it to his mouth, pulled the string tight, then spoke loudly and clearly into it.

'This is Harry Beales of two-two-two Charcoal Street. Please deliver three croissants for my breakfast order, thank you.'

'So, what, it's just another version of your meal-ordering thing?' asked Callum.

'And *more*,' said Harry with a smug smile.

Harry put the first cup back down on the desk, then picked up the second.

'This is Harry Beales of two-two-two Charcoal Street, please deliver two pairs of jeans, two red T-shirts and two grey hoodies, one set for a thirteen-year-old boy and the other for an eleven-year-old. Thank you.'

Harry put the second cup down, then picked up the third and asked for his usual grocery order to be delivered at 6 p.m. that evening. When he was finished, he turned to Adam and Callum and held his hands out, as if he were waiting for a round of applause, or at least some more 'Whoa!'s or 'Amazing!'s. But instead he got –

'That ...' began Adam.

'Is ...' continued Callum.

'A little bit ... erm ... well ... kind of ...

err …' they both bumbled and muttered in a messy cacophony of unimpressedness.

'I wasn't just talking into a cup, you must understand!' Harry quickly explained to Adam. 'This is the *InterNAL*. These pieces of string stretch over *one hundred* metres, all the way to the Meal Kitchen, the clothing store and the supermarket! And someone else was at the other end! With their own transceiver, listening to every word I said. They could even talk back to me if they wanted! Something like, "I'm sorry, Mr Beales, we only have those hoodies in green, will that be OK?" And I would say, "Yes, that would be fine," and they would say, "OK, goodbye to you, sir," and I would say, "And goodbye to you too." We're going to put these into every home in town! Maybe even the country! Maybe even the *world*! Just like your InterNET, yes?'

'Err … well … not *exactly* like the internet,' Adam tried to explain, doing his best not to burst Harry's bubble. 'I mean … wait, in our meeting, that model you showed me of the globe covered in string – the World Wide Web – that wasn't an example of how the InterNAL was going to create a network across the world, it was an actual *model* of how you're going to wrap an actual web of string all around the world?'

'Exactly! We can send these strings *anywhere* – to the library, where someone could *read a book to you* down the line, or even to the concert hall, where you could listen to live music through the InterNAL instead of sitting in a room with thousands of other people!'

'Wait, *what?*' said Callum, his nose crinkled in confusion. 'You like being lonely, but you also go to *concerts?* How does *that* make any sense?'

'It makes perfect sense,' said Harry, with a shrug. 'I mean, leaving the house is never ideal, but concerts are the most acceptable form of communal gatherings – nobody is allowed to talk, you only see the backs of other people's heads, and everyone has their own cubicle of course. It's one of the few things, other than work, that people will actually leave their homes for. But with the InterNAL, they won't even need to do that! The possibilities are endless! People will never need to leave their homes for *anything*! It could be a Nice and Lonely revolution!'

'But no one will ever get to know each other!' Adam protested. 'The world will be such a miserable place!'

'Aha! But that's the beauty of it!' said Harry, clapping his hands together with excitement. 'No one will know if anyone else is miserable, because no one will see each other! We won't have to see each other's misery ever again!'

'This altiverse really needs to meet our mum,' said Callum. 'She'd be doing her "problem shared is a problem halved" thing all over the place!'

'Problem shared ...?' Harry muttered in utter bafflement. 'That is the strangest thing I have ever ... Sorry, won't be a moment!'

Harry grabbed one of the fifteen boxes of Tear-sues that littered his apartment, turned his back on Adam and Callum, then sobbed, non-stop for two whole minutes, before taking a deep breath and turning back to the brothers, with a satisfied smile on his face.

'Ahhhh, that's better! Where were we? What was I saying?'

'Are ... you OK?' asked Adam as he and Callum stared at Harry with intense concern.

'Fine! Why?'

'Er, because, like, you just cried your heart out for, like, two whole minutes!' Callum pointed out. 'Or didn't you realise?'

'I'm confused,' said Harry. 'Why would *crying* mean I'm not all right? Is this another alternate universe differential?'

'*Definitely*,' Adam assured him.

'Are you telling me that people don't *cry* in your universe?'

'No! People *do* cry!' explained Adam. 'Don't get me wrong, crying is a *great* thing – letting your emotions out instead of bottling them up – it's just that we don't really need to cry very much. We definitely don't need to have a little sob-fest in the middle of a regular conversation.'

'How often *do* people cry in the altiverse?' asked Callum.

'Ohh, I don't know, it varies really,' Harry said, scratching his head. 'Probably somewhere between five to fifteen times a day, depending on the person.'

'Wow,' said Callum.

'That is quite a lot,' said Adam. 'Do you think

that maybe people only cry so much *because* they're lonely?'

Harry laughed, as if this was the silliest question he'd ever heard.

'Of course we cry because we're lonely! Just like we eat because we're hungry! Just like we sweat because we're hot! What's your point?'

'Well … I guess my point is … sweating and eating don't make people feel *unhappy*. We eat and sweat because we *have to*, it's part of life, but being lonely doesn't have to be.'

Harry smiled.

'That is something that has never even crossed my mind, Adam. What a brilliant hypothesis. But, right now, I don't think you have time to be trying to fix *our* problems! You have quite a big problem of your own to deal with!'

'Yeah,' Adam groaned, slumping himself into a chair as the difficulty of their situation weighed down on him. 'You're right. And now that it turns out that your InterNAL is just a bunch of tin cups and string, and isn't actually *anything like* the internet, I think I could probably sob for ten minutes straight, because the InterNAL is *definitely* not going to help us get home.'

Harry passed Adam a box of Tear-sues.

'Thanks,' said Adam, placing them back on a table. 'I wasn't meaning *literally*.'

'Don't lose heart, Adam,' Harry said encouragingly. 'I have a whole bunch of ideas to get you two back home!'

'You do?' Adam and Callum both gasped in wide-eyed hope.

'Of course I do! Wait right there!'

At first, when Harry reappeared holding an abacus, with a stick strapped to his head, saying, 'So you say it was all done with a computer and a memory stick, yes?' Adam didn't hold up much hope of ever getting home. But the more they explained about Popularis, and computers and the internet, the closer they came to finding a solution. And so began the whirlwind of non-stop experiments to get Adam and Callum back home.

DAY ONE

'I don't understand why we had to do this so *early*,'

yawned Callum as Harry, wearing the biggest backpack known to man, unlocked a side door of Stephington Industries and the three of them stepped quietly into the deserted building.

'Because we are attempting to recreate your dimensional leap, to the *exact* detail,' Harry explained for the fifth time that morning. 'You travelled *here*, to this altiverse, at sunrise, so we will try to send you *back* at sunrise. You travelled from office A21, so we will try to send you *back* from office A21. And everything else has to be as similar as possible to how it was at the moment you were transported here – the memory stick, the screen, the sense of impending doom, the argument. If we can replicate it to perfection, we might also be able to replicate the transportation to another universe.'

'I have no idea what you're talking about.' Callum yawned again. 'You lost me at the part where you said … words.'

'Basically, you know that morning when we got zapped into this altiverse?' said Adam, attempting to explain it in simpler terms. 'Well, we're going to try to do all of that stuff again, to see if it'll zap us back home.'

'But we don't have a *computer*,' said Callum. 'I thought that was the whole point!'

'Your phone is going to stand in for the computer,' explained Adam as the trio stepped into office A21 and Adam placed Callum's phone on the desk, in the exact spot the computer had been back in their universe.

'What happens if people decide to come to work early today? Won't we get in trouble?' asked Callum.

'No one will come to work early because today is *Friday*, Callum,' said Harry. 'The first day of the weekend.'

'You have your weekends on Friday and Saturday?'

'*And* Sunday,' Harry corrected him. 'After four days in other people's company, we need some decent "me time" at the weekend.'

'I'm really beginning to like this altiverse!'

Harry pulled his gigantic backpack off and began assembling something in the corner of the room.

'So, we're in the right location, at the right time,

we've got the memory stick, we've got the computer-type-thing, and I ... will provide ... the sense ... of IMPENDING DOOM!' Harry spun round and held aloft the object he had so painstakingly assembled.

'It's a fake Christmas tree,' said Adam. 'I'm confused.'

'You said that a tree fell through the roof,' said Harry. 'This is the tree!'

Harry climbed on to a chair and held the tree high above Adam's and Callum's heads.

'Now argue!'

'What?' said Callum.

'You told me you were arguing when you got transported here,' Harry reminded them, 'so now you have to argue again.'

'About what?' laughed Adam. 'We can't just start arguing about nothing!'

'You two seem to be *experts* at arguing over nothing,' Harry assured them. 'Give it a go.'

'We *can't*!' Adam insisted. 'It doesn't work like that! Arguments are things that build up over time, and then they just ...'

'You smell,' Callum suddenly blurted at Adam.

'Is that your lame attempt at starting an argument?' Adam asked. 'Because it's not going to work.'

'Better than *your* attempt, smelly pants.'

'Trust me, if I wanted to start an argument, I could do a lot better than "smelly pants".'

'No you couldn't.'

'Yes, I could. And, for a start, I would …'

'SMELLY PANTS!'

'You are *so* immature.'

'No I'm not.'

'This isn't even an argument, it's just you saying stupid …'

'*You're* immature.'

'You can't *force* an argument just by being annoying, Callum, it …'

'THE TREE IS GOING TO FALL!' Harry bellowed, shaking the Christmas tree above their heads.

Adam was not impressed.

'Harry, I think—'

'You smell?' Callum interrupted. '*I* think you smell too.'

'Guys, come on! This isn't working. We need to …'

'THE TREE IS GOING TO CRUSH YOU!'

'This is the bit where Adam is supposed to start crying like a baby!' said Callum. '"*I want to go home! I want my mummy!*"'

'It's not funny, Callum, we *do* need to go home! We need to let Mum know we're all right! She'll be worried sick about us!'

'We're staying!' yelled Callum. 'Stop crying!'

'I can't even tell if you're being serious right now, Cal, but it's Mum's birthday in *three days*, and she …'

'WAAAAA! WAAAA! WAAAA! It's *MY* wish, Adam! It's up to me! And I say we're STAYING!'

'We're NOT staying!'

'I'M GOING TO DROP IT ON YOUR HEADS!'

'Harry, shut up!' Adam said.

'You shut up, Adam!' Callum bellowed. 'Don't talk to Dad like that! You're not the boss here!'

'I don't even know what's going on right now!'

'TREEEEEEEE!' roared Harry. 'FALLING TREEEEEE!'

'This is stupid. I'm going.'

'You're STAYING!'

Callum grabbed Adam's pyjama top.

'No, Callum, I'm going!'

'You'll *ruin it*, Adam!'

'Callum, I ...'

'TRRREEEEEEEE!'

And Harry threw the fake tree down and then ...!

Adam stood there, with a big fake Christmas tree bent across his head, while Callum doubled over in silent laughter.

'I'm pretty sure ...' Adam growled through gritted teeth, 'that *didn't work*.'

DAY TWO

Adam and Callum trekked from Ethan's to Harry's once again, and this time they spent the day focusing on technical experiments to get them home. Experiments like trying to wirelessly connect the memory stick to Callum's phone, or trying to plug the memory stick into a calculator, or the slightly less technical moment where Harry tried rubbing the memory stick, hoping to coax the genie out of

it. 'Like the little girl did in that "Alassin" story!'
But by the end of the day, Adam and Callum were
trudging back to Ethan's shed, with heads full of
worry, hearts low on hope and phone even lower on
battery.

DAY THREE

Harry had cleared a space in his apartment big
enough to use as a laboratory, but the day's experiments felt rushed and desperate, with Harry
attempting to use magnets to transfer the data
from the memory stick into the phone, or trying,
once again, to awaken Popularis with more
arguments, more wishes and even more realistic
moments of impending doom. And the day ended
with Adam and Callum leaving early, and Harry
promising he'd never lock them in a room with a
poisonous snake without their permission ever
again.

'Tomorrow! After work! I'll have it cracked!' he
called down the street after them. 'I promise!'

After three days of non-stop experiments, Adam
and Callum weren't sure they would ever get back

home. But on their way back to Ethan's, a completely different solution was presented to them.

'Adam, is that car following us?' Callum whispered.

'Definitely,' Adam confirmed.

The driver of the car was doing their best to hang back, crawling slowly along behind them, hoping not to be noticed. But since there wasn't a single other car out on the streets of Derry, it stuck out like a car-sized sore thumb.

'Let's walk faster,' Adam suggested.

But as the brothers picked up speed, so did the car.

'This is getting creepy,' complained Callum.

'Let's try to lose them. When I say "go", we're going to break left, into this park, and run as fast as we can to the other side. OK? Three ... two ... one ... GO!'

As the brothers went sprinting across a playing field, the car was unable to follow. It slammed on its brakes, lurched forward, as if trying to decide what to do, then it too went racing off. Adam and Callum didn't slacken the pace. They carried on, as fast as they could, out the other end of the park, down a small side street, on to a winding residential road, cutting through a narrow back alley, then out on to another road, just minutes away from Ethan's house.

'I think we did it!' Adam exclaimed, as they both paused to catch their breath. 'I think we lost them!'

And that's when the car came screeching to a halt in front of them, and the driver's side window slid down.

'Whoa! Whoa! Whoa! You don't need to panic! I'm here to help!' the driver quickly blurted, holding his hands in the air as if that proved he was harmless.

But Adam only had to take one look at him to know that he wasn't telling the truth.

'I know who you are!' Adam yelled. 'You're Stan Kilter! Your wife tried to steal our phone! And you haven't done anything to help me or my brother your whole life!'

'Well, you may be right,' Bruce's dad admitted. 'But I didn't say I was here to help *you*. I'm here to help your dad. My *friend*. All I want to do is talk.

You don't have to trust me. In fact, you *shouldn't* trust me; I'm a grown man who just chased you in his car! I'd be disappointed in you if you *did* trust me. But if I stay in my car, and you stay over there, please will you listen to what I have to say? Two minutes, that's all I ask.'

'Fine,' said Adam begrudgingly.

Two minutes would probably be just long enough for the two of them to get their breath back, ready to start running again, should they need to.

'Thank you. Right. First of all, my wife, Steph, sends her apologies for scaring you the other day. She saw your disguises, saw a piece of tech that she assumed had been stolen from her lab, and she jumped to conclusions. She thought you were a pair of thieves. Con artists. Partly due to the striking similarities you bear to a pair of boys who appeared at Stephington Industries earlier in the week, just seemed to materialised out of thin air before running amok throughout the building, frightening the living daylights out of our staff.'

'So much for those disguises, then,' Callum muttered from the corner of his mouth.

'But now we know better,' Mr Kilter continued. 'Bruce explained the whole situation to us, and, well, we're willing to put the past behind us, if you are? I'm sure you understand. Secondly, and you probably won't be pleased to hear this, but, these past few evenings, Harry has been stopping by at our VZ, also explaining your situation to us, so that we might help with ideas on how to fix your predicament – that you're lost, and he's helping to get you back home. Something like that, right?'

'One minute left,' said Callum, pretending to check an imaginary watch on his wrist.

'But what he won't explain to us is why, in these past few days, being around you two has made him the happiest I've ever seen him. It's weird. But it's good. Good for *him*. He could do with being happy. All I'm saying is … what's the rush? Do you really need to get back home right away?'

'Yes,' said Adam, with as much force as he could muster. 'We do.'

'What if you decided to stick around a bit longer?' Stan continued as if he hadn't heard Adam. 'What's the hurry, eh? You'd get to spend a bit more time with Harry, Harry would get to spend a bit more time with you, and in the meantime, we could get a whole team of our people at Stephington Industries to help you find a way back home. I bet, with that little device of yours, with the moving photographs and what have you, *anything's* possible. And if we could learn a little bit more about your technology, it could make Harry a very rich man. What do you say?'

The answer was simple.

'That ...' said Adam.

'Is ...' continued Callum.

'*Stupid!*' concluded Adam at exactly the same time as Callum said –

'*Genius!*'

Adam glared at Callum as though he had literally stabbed him in the back.

'Good, good!' Stan grinned, again as if he hadn't heard Adam. 'Glad you boys are on board. How about you swing by the office tomorrow, and we'll have our best scientists have a look at that device of yours? We can have an entire team of scientists working on this! Better to take our time and do it properly than to rush it and mess it up, wouldn't you agree? And who knows, before too long we might be able to build another one of your devices! Or maybe even one of your "computers" I've heard so much about!'

'Deal!' said Callum, looking as if he'd just been offered free ice cream for life.

'Absolutely not,' growled Adam.

'Great stuff!' cheered Stan, as he began slowly

driving away. 'Let's say nine a.m.! I'll have breakfast waiting for you!'

And then he was gone.

Adam and Callum were left alone, standing at the mouth of the back alley, about to have the biggest disagreement of their lives.

11

The Beginning of a
Beautiful Friendship

Adam awoke with a croaky throat and a dry cough, probably as a result of all the shouting and arguing he and Callum had done the previous evening. And night. And early hours of that morning. And even though they had both eventually skulked off to their separate corners of the shed and got some sleep, Adam still woke up feeling angry. The argument lingered in the shed like a smaller version of the huge thundercloud that loomed outside. Like a fart trapped under a duvet. Like an egg in a microwave, waiting to explode.

Adam couldn't believe that Callum could be so

stupid! That he could want to agree with Stan Kilter instead of his own brother! That he could risk everything just so that he could selfishly have a slightly longer altiverse holiday! Adam had tried everything, but it had proved to be an argument he couldn't win. Callum was determined to be at Stephington Industries at 9 o'clock sharp.

Adam tried to swallow his anger. He took a deep breath, nestled his head back into his big, orange Cuddle Gnome, and he stared at the wooden wall, wishing he were in his own bed, with his own pillow, staring at his own wall, listening to Mum clattering around downstairs.

Mum.

He wondered what she was doing right now. He tried to imagine how worried she must be about them, but the ache in his chest was too unbearable.

'You're still wrong.' Adam jolted in his sleeping bag at the shock of hearing Callum's croaky voice. 'We *can* stay here longer.'

'Callum, how can you be so selfish? Think about Mum!' Adam growled with fury.

'How can *you* be so selfish?!' Callum snapped

back. 'We get to spend our whole lives with Mum! This is the only time we get to spend with Dad! Once we're home, that's it, we never see him again! Ever!'

'And if your battery runs down, we have no screen, and that means no Popularis, and that means we won't ever see *Mum* again, ever!'

'Adam, you heard what he said, Mr Kilter, we'd be working with their best scientists! I'm pretty sure they'll figure out how to recharge a phone battery!'

'Or blow it up. Cal, our technology is completely alien to them. They have no idea what they're doing!'

'And here we go again.' Callum sighed bitterly. 'Everything has to be what *Adam* wants, because stupid little Callum doesn't count!'

'Callum! Stan Kilter cannot be trusted! Steph Kilter cannot be trusted! None of the Kilters can be trusted! End of!'

'But maybe they *can*. Some things are different in this altiverse, Adam, in case you hadn't noticed.'

'Fine!' Adam kicked his sleeping bag off. 'You want to trust them? Let's go. Let's go to Stephington

Industries. Let's walk straight into their trap. And when they take our phone, and we end up stuck here forever, it'll be all your fault!' What was the point of trying to protect Callum when he didn't want protecting?

'Fine!' agreed Callum, kicking his own sleeping bag off. 'Because you know what, Adam? You're not always right about everything! And you know what else? It's not *our* phone, it's *my* phone, and I'll do what I like with it!'

Their exit from Ethan's garden was swift: no using the silly button-tastic ordering machine for breakfast, no bothering to tell Ethan where they were going, and not a single word more exchanged between the two of them. For once they managed to stay quiet for the entire bus journey, each in their own cubicle, staring angrily at the framed advertisements on the walls. Today all the ads were the same – a picture of a box of tissues with a sales pitch beneath it – 'Taylor's Tear-sues: the finest Solitary Sob Sheets, with added moisturisers and anti-inflammatories to reduce redness and puffiness.'

Callum's going to be needing those when Stan Kilter ruins the rest of our lives, Adam growled inwardly.

They stepped through the doors of Stephington Industries at exactly 9 a.m., and both Stan and Steph Kilter were right there, waiting for them.

'Oh, yes! I'm so glad you came!' Steph cheered, with a clap of her hands. 'So glad we get to start things afresh after such a regrettable first meeting. Stan did explain my unforgiveable outburst, I hope? Oh, I'm so embarrassed, chasing you poor things from the meeting like that. You must think I'm a *complete monster*!'

'It's fine,' Callum assured her with a little laugh. 'We must have looked kind of bananas ourselves.'

Stan and Steph both howled with laughter at Callum's 'banana' pun, throwing their heads back and clapping their hands.

'Oh dear, oh dear,' sighed Stan as he wiped the laughter from his eyes. 'You truly are as wise as you both look! How lucky we are to have you here. Please do follow me, gentlemen, this way!'

The Kilters bombarded Adam and Callum with small-talk questions about their health, the weather and how well they slept last night. But Adam wasn't listening, because up on the first floor, as they made their way across the concourse, he spotted someone who caused him to break out in a hot sweat.

Adam poked Callum in the back and squeezed his hand. Callum looked at him pitifully.

'Adam, I know you're mad at me, but violence is never the answer.'

'No, you dope!' He struggled to keep his voice down. 'Look! It's MUM! Or the other mother. Or our alti-mum. Whatever you want to call her, she's heading straight towards us!'

Callum swivelled his curly-haired bean head to the side, trying not to look obvious while simultaneously looking *really* obvious.

'YIKES! What's SHE doing here?! She thinks we're criminals who broke into her house! If she sees us we're toast! Like, "arrested-by-altiverse-police" type of toast!'

'SSSSHHHH!' whispered Adam.

'Everything all good here?' Stan peered over his shoulder mid-walk, with an unnatural spring in his step. 'We're heading to the research laboratory, which is just towards the back of the building. Not far now.'

'Yeah, so that's very interesting artwork there. French, I'd say late nineteenth century . . .' Callum spoke in an English accent, while pointing to, well . . . umm, a toilet door, 180 degrees from Mum's location.

'Callum, what the actual heck are you *doing*?'

'Follow my lead, Adam, you numpty, she's right there! Our heads, this way!' Callum gave Adam wide eyes and drew his attention to the series of non-existent artworks in the other direction, averting their faces.

'Oh, right,' muttered Adam, finally cottoning on to Callum's clumsy plan before adopting his own version of an English accent and hoping for the best.

'Oh my word, look at this sculpture – so contemporary, so simple, so . . . illuminating,' he added, as he paused to admire a . . . erm, a light switch.

It worked. Altiverse-Mum sailed straight past, completely oblivious, and Adam couldn't help but silently giggle. *How does he do it?* Adam wondered to himself. *Callum still manages to make me laugh even when I can't stand the sight of him!*

'And here we are, boys – our very own research lab!' announced Steph Kilter with a chirpiness that sounded about as natural as a whistling lion. 'In we go!'

Stan swung a pair of doors open to reveal a room that didn't look too different from a school science lab, except instead of being full of motor-mouthed kids, this place was full of techy-looking science nerds in white coats. One scientist, who looked as though he'd hopped straight out of a comic book – frizzy white hair, giant specs, huge moustache – stepped forward and introduced himself.

'Goot mornink! I am Professor Frederick Arty-Facće, ant I vill be leading the reverse enchineerink of your little dootle-votsit. I can tell just by looking at you zat ve are goink to be great friends.'

'Erm …' Adam had no idea what the man had just said, or even what he'd said his name was, so he took a quick look at the man's name tag. 'Nice to meet you, Prof—'

But that was as far as Adam could get, because when he saw the name written on the man's little plastic badge, the world's biggest snort of laughter got caught in the back of his throat.

OK, so *technically* the badge read *Professor F. Arty-Facće*, but come on! You didn't have to have a ridiculously childish brain like Adam's for it to look a lot like —

> *Professor Farty Face*

Adam bit his lip and tried to hold back his laughter. And he was convinced he would have managed it, had it not been for one thing —

The quivering whimper that wibbled from Callum's lips. He'd spotted the name tag too.

Adam struggled valiantly onwards. 'Hmmm … nice to … mm-eeeheee …'

The laugh was bubbling low in his stomach.

'… to meheeet you … Professor Faaaaa … Haaaaaaa …'

It was coming! The laughter eruption was on its way and there was nothing he could do to stop it!

'Mr Faaaaaa-haaaaaaa … haaaaaaaaa …'

'Are you qvuite all right, Mr Bealies?'

Beside him, Callum was turning red and making a high-pitched whining noise from his nose.

'Vould you like a glass of vater? Or perhaps a teeny veeny cup of Conker-Juice Tea?'

That was it! It was too much! The laughter exploded from Adam's face with an almighty –

'BAAAAAAAAAAAAAAAAAHAAAAAAAAAAA!!!'

Professor Farty Face leaped back in surprise. Adam did his best to disguise his outburst.

'HAAAAAA-HA-HA-HOWWWW kind of you! Yes! Please! We love Conker-Juice Tea! Mmmm! Our favourite! Yummy, right, Callum?'

But Callum couldn't speak. He was pinching his nose and lips shut while violently shaking with the effort of holding back his own laughter.

'Oh,' said Professor Farty Face, taking a few nervous steps backwards. 'Err ... gooty gooty. Vould you also like a plate of biscvuits? Ve have my favourites – Clown-fish Liver Svirly-Vhirlies.'

Despite all being verified geniuses, none of the scientists could quite figure out why exactly the two brothers were rolling around on the floor, clutching their stomachs and laughing so hard they were in danger of dying.

'Do excuse them,' Stan Kilter said to the scientists. 'They're not from around here. Perhaps we could all take a seat at the table?'

This last comment was mainly directed towards Adam and Callum, who nodded in agreement, then feebly crawled over to a long workbench, dragging themselves into a pair of chairs while they continued to silently cry with laughter.

Once they'd managed to dry their eyes, they looked up to find two dozen faces all staring at them in confusion.

'Sorry,' said Adam, trying to straighten up. 'It's just that we're so happy to be here.'

'And we're happy to have you here.' Stan beamed insincerely.

'So,' said Steph, clearing her throat as if to announce that business had begun. 'I've been telling my team here about your little device, the one with the moving photographs. Do you mind?' She gestured to Callum's pocket, where his phone was peeking out.

'Oh, yeah, sure.' Callum pulled out his phone and the room fell silent. 'Ah, sorry, powered it off to save battery life.' He held the side button for a few seconds until the screen lit up, tapped the four-digit passcode and then passed it towards Steph's outstretched hand.

Adam was definitely not laughing any more.

'Perhaps you should give a quick demonstration first, Callum,' Adam suggested. 'Show everyone what it can do?'

'Brilliant idea,' said Steph, forcing a smile as she snatched her hand back, which Adam had noticed was trembling with anticipation.

'Ah, so, here, look.' Callum turned the phone around and showed the room.

He swiped through the various home screens, photographs and any apps that didn't require an internet connection, but Adam wasn't paying Callum much mind. He was too busy watching the audience. The scientists were all out of their seats, leaning closer, their eyes wide with disbelief. They muttered in amazement, gawped with fascination, and when Callum opened his car racing game, some of them gasped with shock.

But it was Mr and Mrs Kilter who really had

Adam's attention. They too were watching on with bulging eyes, but every now and then they shared a greedy look of satisfaction, like two gamblers who knew they had bet on the right horse.

'So,' said Adam, putting an abrupt halt to the screen-show, 'about you helping to get us home?'

'Truly astounding ...' said Stan Kilter, still staring at the phone with heat-seeking eyeballs.

'Think of the possibilities ...' added Steph, as if she'd been hypnotised.

'Yeah, soooooo, home? Us?' Adam tried again.

'It could revolutionise the entire world ...' muttered Stan, still transfixed. Adam nudged Callum's arm.

'Stop swiping!' he hissed.

'Oh, sure, yeah.' Callum spun the phone around and clicked the side button, powering off the screen. 'Sorry, guys, battery power and all that.'

SNAP SNAP – Adam clicked his fingers, attempting to break Stan and Steph's trance.

'So you think you can do it? Get us home?'

'Ah yes, home? Yes, of course, home ...' Stan blinked as if he'd just woken from a deep sleep.

'With technology like that I'm sure we could send you *anywhere*,' added Steph, flashing her Cheshire-cat smile.

'Absolutely!' cheered Stan, almost fully alert now. 'If we could just, ermmm … have it for a few days, I'm sure we could have a look at how it works, replicate its technology, strip out the design, redesign, repurpose …'

'Well, the first thing you'll need to do is recharge the battery,' said Adam. 'Do you know how to do that?'

'My dear boy, do not vorry yourself, ve have ze *greatest* understanding of how battereeze work!' laughed Professor Arty-Facće. 'Vhy, I charged a battery viz five whole volts of electricity just yesterday, simply by immersing it in a tub of eight hundred electric eels. It iz child's play, believe me!'

'You want to charge the battery by putting the phone in a tub of water, filled with eels?' asked Adam, numb with horror at what he was hearing.

'How else?' laughed another scientist.

Callum held the phone tight to his chest.

'Errr … I think maybe I'll hold on to it a little while longer.'

Adam and Callum both slid out of their seats and began backing away, towards the doors, but the scientists moved in, swarming around them.

'Boys, boys, let's be reasonable now! A deal is a deal!' Stan declared, pulling a key from his pocket as he attempted to head them off at the doors.

'Except we didn't do any deal, did we?' said Adam, trying to force his way through the scientists.

'Oh, children, have a little faith!' Steph insisted, smiling coldly as she inched towards them. 'We have the smartest scientific minds in the world, right here in this room! There's no problem they can't fix!'

'Well,' said Callum, still backing away, 'they might be the smartest minds in *this* universe, but where we come from they're totally …'

'Cracked!' boomed a voice from the doorway.

Every single person in the room gasped as the doors flew open, and they all turned to see …

'Harry?' Stan cried in alarm. 'What are you …?'

'I've cracked it! I know how to recharge the battery! Give me one day with that phone and it will be running at full capacity!'

'Are you certain about this, Harry?' asked Steph, sounding more than a little sceptical.

'*Absolutely* certain,' Harry assured her. 'But we haven't a second to lose. If the battery drains completely, there is nothing I can do. It will be lost forever.'

'Fine,' Steph reluctantly agreed. 'But have it back here, in this room, first thing tomorrow morning. Agreed?'

'I shall have it safely returned before you even know it,' Harry assured her.

And then they were off – Adam, Callum and Harry were out of the door and making their way back across the building.

'You did it! You figured out a way to charge the battery?' Callum panted as the brothers jogged to keep up with Harry's energetic stride.

'Nope.'

'No? But you just told them ...'

'I told them what I *needed* to tell them in order to get you two out of there.'

'So I was right, wasn't I?' Adam almost cheered with self-satisfaction. 'We can't trust them, can we?'

'Stan and Steph?' asked Harry. 'It's not them I'm worried about. I was actually on my way to ask for their help with our research, but ... seeing who they've hired, I'm not so sure about that any more. Something about your phone has got them acting very peculiarly, that's for sure. You see, the scientists in that room are *not* regular Stephington staff. They are a team of outside scientists who do not have a good reputation. I'm sure Stan and Steph don't know this, but not a single one of their new scientists can be trusted. Bad eggs, the lot of them. One of them spent time in jail for sneaking adverts for his weapons company into children's books. Another made a fortune when he opened the Speedy Gambling booths, which led to *millions* of people losing *all* their money in a matter of *minutes*. And possibly the worst of them all, Professor Arty-Facće, invented a sausage that has now been banned from the meal-ordering menu ...'

'Because they were poisoned?' guessed Callum.

'Because they were filled with addictive ingredients?' guessed Adam.

'That's the thing,' explained Harry. 'They were

just ordinary, rubbish sausages. But it got to a point where it was the only food the Meal Kitchen was offering! Every day! For every meal! Because he hypnotised everybody into wanting to eat his sausages and nothing else!'

'No way!' gasped Callum. 'Did he get arrested?'

'They tried, but he hypnotised the police. And even if they *could* have arrested him, he'd never have gone to jail because he would just hypnotise the judge and the jury. And even if they *could* get him in jail, he'd just hypnotise the prison guards to let him straight back out again!'

'An evil genius,' Callum whispered in awe.

'Every last one of them,' Harry confirmed. 'So when I saw Stan and Steph were taking you in for a meeting with them I knew I had to get you out of there and keep your phone as far away from them as possible.'

'So, when you said you would return the phone, you were lying, right?' asked Adam.

'Not lying, Adam. I told the exact truth. I *will* return the phone, first thing tomorrow ... back to its rightful home, in its rightful universe, with its rightful owners!'

'You mean … you've figured it out?!' Adam gasped. 'You know how to get us home?'

Harry paused in the doorway, on his way out of the building, and turned to the boys with a big smile on his face and a twinkle in his eye.

'Follow me, boys, and prepare to be amazed.'

And then he walked straight into a lady with her arms full of notebooks and folders, and they both went crashing to the floor in a fluttering shower of paper.

'I am *so* sorry!' Harry grunted as he got to his feet, reached out a hand to help the flustered lady back up, then slipped on her papers and landed flat on his face, again.

'Oh, no, *I'm* sorry. It was just as much my fault!' the lady insisted as she got up and heaved Harry back to his feet. 'I was too busy staring at these boys, wondering where I'd seen them before!'

Since she was no longer covered in a deluge of paper, Adam and Callum finally got a good look at her, and they both turned white as sheets when they realised who it was …

'Mum!' Callum blurted before he could stop himself.

'Yeah!' Adam quickly jumped in. 'Mum … err … Mum … *Mama mia!* What a mess!'

There she was, right in front of them, staring directly at the two of them – their very own mum. And this time she wasn't screaming, calling the police, or accusing them of being aliens, which was a big relief. Their alti-mum, alongside their alti-dad.

It was like an alti-family reunion! And there seemed to be a little stare-a-thon going on. Dad was staring at Mum, Mum was staring at Dad, Adam and Callum were staring at *both of them,* and they all had dopey smiles on their faces. Then, at exactly the same time, all four of them seemed to realise that they were each staring, and quickly busied them-selves by gathering up the hundreds of sheets of paper from the floor.

'Lovely to meet, you,' said Harry, clumsily drop-ping every piece of paper he'd just picked up. 'I'm Harry, by the way.'

'Edelle,' said alti-Mum, reaching out to shake Harry's hand, and causing him to drop everything he'd picked up again. And then she turned her

attention to Adam and Callum, eyeing them curiously. 'You two *do* seem very familiar. Have we met before?'

'No!' Callum replied a little too quickly and much too loudly. 'You probably recognise us because we're YouTubers!'

Adam winced. Callum had been so quick to come up with a lie that he'd totally neglected to remember that YouTube didn't exist here.

'YouTubers?' she repeated, looking puzzled.

'We're in a band!' Adam quickly explained. 'A two-man brass band. We both play tubas. We're called You Tubas. We're quite famous … in other countries.'

Her eyes narrowed as if the memory of where she'd seen them before was returning to her, when Harry distracted her by handing back her huge stack of papers.

'There you go! That's all of them, I think,' he said with a smile.

'Oh, thank you. Thank you all!'

'No worries,' said Adam, breathing a huge sigh of relief as she turned to leave.

'A problem shared is a problem halved,' said Callum.

She paused, turned back to Callum and stared at him curiously.

'Ignore him,' said Adam quickly. 'He says weird things like that. He's not from around here.'

Adam was worried that she was about to tell Callum off for being so disrespectful of the NAL way of life, but she didn't. Instead she smiled, and said, 'I like that. I've never heard anything like that before, but I like it.'

'Yeah, err, my mum used to say it all the time,' said Callum.

'Very wise,' she said. 'I like your mum.'

And then she left.

Adam spotted one of her sheets of paper that was still under his foot, and he called after her.

'Wait! You missed one!'

But it was too late. She was already getting on a bus, with the doors closing behind her.

Adam picked the paper up. It looked like a boring spreadsheet of sales figures and expenses, but then he noticed that all of her details were printed at the top of the page:

Miss E. Crawley
CEO, BusScribers Advertising
Floor 4, Lowers House
Stephington Lane, Derry

And this gave Adam an idea. *Maybe I could get alti-Mum and alti-Dad together! Like a couple! Like ... who knows, maybe even one day they might get married! And have kids!* The thought of making Harry a little less 'nice and lonely' sent a spark of joy zipping through Adam's veins. And the thought that he might set off an interdimensional domino effect that could potentially result in the creation of an alti-Adam and alti-Callum made him feel undeniably almighty – and a little bit icky at the same time.

'It's on headed paper, with her business address and everything. You could, maybe, I don't know, just drop it off for her one day, Harry.'

'Ah, good idea, Adam,' said Harry, snatching the paper from Adam's grip a little too eagerly. 'I'll be sure to do that.'

'So, I get why we can't tell *her* that she's our mum, but we can tell Harry, right?' Callum whispered.

'No!' Adam whispered back. 'We can't mess around with stuff like that. Harry *likes* her! Couldn't you tell by the way he looked at her? If we go telling him that in our universe they got married and had kids, that could totally freak him out! They might never get together! But if we leave it, it looks like the universe might bring them together all by itself. Well, maybe with a *tiny* bit of help from me.'

Adam and Callum watched, with knowing smirks, as Harry carefully folded the sheet of paper and put it in his inside pocket, next to his heart.

'So ... are we witnessing the beginning of a beautiful friendship?' Callum whispered.

'I think we might be!' Adam giggled in reply.

'Are you two interested in getting home or not?' Harry called as he marched towards the bus stop. 'Because I really *do* have something amazing to show you!'

12

Wakey Wakey, Popularis!

As Adam and Callum stood in the centre of Harry's cathedral-like apartment, waiting for Harry to explain his amazing discovery, Adam found that he couldn't stop himself from shaking with anticipation. It felt like every Christmas morning, waiting to unwrap his presents, every theme park queue, just as he was about to get on the roller coaster, every school sports day, just before they would fire the starting pistol for the running race – all of those things rolled into one.

He's actually figured it out! Adam kept telling himself. *We're finally going to go back home! He's done it! He's … he's … he's taking so long to explain it!*

'Let me just, ah, move this over here,' Harry

blustered as he continued shifting all of his inventions to the edges of the room, 'and, er, yes, better get this coffee cup out of the way, then … Where was I? Oh, just one minute, I might need to pop to the loo, and …'

'Harry, *please*, the suspense is literally killing me!' Adam moaned.

'I suppose the toilet can wait a few minutes. Yes. Right. OK. I'm ready.'

Harry was standing next to the only item in his apartment that hadn't been pushed to the edge of the room – a large table with a blanket thrown over the top of it – where he nervously addressed Adam and Callum as if he were hosting a very small press conference.

'It happened last night, you see. I kept going over everything you told me about how the internet works, how it's a never-ending source of information and entertainment. And then I thought about what you told me about Popularis – how it needs the internet in order to exist. And just by putting those two pieces of information together, I figured out *how* Popularis works!'

Adam and Callum were waiting in silence, hoping Harry would come to the part where he *showed* them that he'd got Popularis up and running, but Harry just stood there, staring at the brothers with an expectant grin on his face, and Adam realised that this was where he was supposed to say something encouraging.

'Wow! That's great, Harry,' he offered. 'And? Did you get it to work?'

'Well … first of all … you were, kind of, supposed to ask *how* it works.'

'Oh, yeah … erm … Wow! So, how *does* Popularis work, Harry?'

'Aha! I'm glad you asked! Well, that's the interesting bit! You see, Popularis is like a *brain* – able to cause an array of amazing physical feats, even think unbelievable thoughts, dream unimaginable dreams – but, like your brain, it needs *blood and oxygen* to function! The *internet* is like the blood and oxygen for Popularis. The internet *feeds* Popularis all of the information it needs in order to make the impossible possible! You see?'

'Err … kind of. I think. Maybe,' said Adam. 'But

where is this going? We still don't have the internet here!'

'No, we don't!' Harry said, almost buzzing with excitement. 'But what is the internet made up of? I said it before – non-stop information and entertainment! We have the brain, right here.' Harry pulled the Popularis source code memory stick from his pocket and held it in front of the brothers' faces. 'All we need to do to bring it to life is to feed it the blood – the information and entertainment!'

'I *know*,' said Adam. 'But how do we do that without the *internet*?'

'You're thinking too *literally*, Adam! You're thinking about how Popularis worked in *your* universe. But the internet isn't the only place that information and entertainment exist! Everything on the internet got there because *people* put it there! The internet didn't *create* the information, *humans* did! The internet was just somewhere for them to *put* their information! Look at this …'

Harry whipped the blanket from the table to reveal … well, just a couple of wires and one of his silver InterNAL cups.

'Oh,' said Callum flatly. 'I was expecting something so much more impressive.'

'That's the thing, Cal, it's *so simple*!'

Harry picked up the silver cup. Adam noticed that connected to the cup was a home-made USB cable, which Harry slotted into the memory stick.

'Took me all night to build that connection,' Harry said, noticing Adam inspecting his handiwork. 'Now, keep looking at that flashing red light on the memory stick.'

Harry picked up his silver cup and began speaking into it.

'My name is Harry Beales, and when I was six years old I fell off my bike and broke three of my fingers. Twelve plus four is sixteen. The sky is blue and grass is green. I'm afraid of balloons. The blue whale is the largest animal ever to exist on earth. A square has four sides ...'

Adam and Callum could barely believe their eyes! The red light on top of the memory stick was no longer blinking. Instead it was *glowing*, bright and steady.

'Callum ...' Adam whispered. 'I think he's actually waking Popularis up!'

'HA HA!' Harry squealed with excitement. 'Now you two join in! Come on!'

Adam and Callum stood either side of Harry as he held the silver cup out for all three of them to speak into.

'What do we tell it?' asked Callum.

'Information, Callum! Information and entertainment! *Facts!* Come on, all of us together!'

So, all at the same time, the three Beales boys began reeling off non-stop pieces of information:

'There are seven colours in a rainbow.'

'My favourite flavour crisps are prawn cocktail.'

'Cheetahs are the fastest land mammals.'

'If you pick your nose too much it will end up bleeding.'

'Humans are the only animals that cry tears of sadness.'

'Six plus six is twelve.'

'$E = mc^2$.'

'The light is getting brighter!'

'The more we speak, the brighter it gets!'

'Popularis is waking up!'

'Callum is going to hand me his phone!'

'This is so exciting I think I might burst!'

'I am going to connect the phone to the memory stick too!'

Harry had made a phone cable out of sixteen wires all attached to a tiny piece of a lollipop stick that had been whittled down to the shape of a charging plug. He picked up the memory stick, and attached one end of the cable to the USB socket, alongside the wires for the tin cup. Then he plugged the other end of the cable into the phone, and the phone gave a chime to acknowledge that something had been plugged into it.

'Is this going to charge the phone up?' asked Callum.

'No, Callum, it's going to charge *Popularis* up! And if we give Popularis enough information, we will see it on your phone! Popularis will do that thing you told me about – your screen will glow white! There will be a high-pitched squeal! Then three bright flashes! And whatever you wish for will come true!'

'Keep going!' cheered Adam. 'More facts! All of us! But faster this time!'

So off they went again, on a high-speed, non-stop, rapid-fire fact marathon. And this time the memory stick glowed twice as bright, for twice as long, but ...

'Nothing's happening,' Callum announced. 'It's not working!'

'Don't stop, Callum!' Adam barked. 'Keep talking! More information! More facts!'

'He hasn't stopped,' Harry sadly admitted. 'That *was* a fact – it's *not* working.'

'But it *was*!' Adam growled with frustration. 'The red light was glowing!'

'Yes,' agreed Harry, 'Popularis was *beginning* to wake up. But it's not enough. We need Popularis to be *wide awake*, singing and dancing and bouncing off the walls. All we managed to do was make it groan, and roll over, and pull the blanket over its head.'

'So we go *quicker*! Louder!' Adam insisted.

'It still won't be enough,' Harry softly explained. 'We just threw, what, fifty, sixty facts at it? But how many facts are in the internet?'

'A few hundred billion?' said Callum. 'A trillion?'

'We need to get closer to those numbers if we really want Popularis at full strength. A few thousand, at *least*.'

'But *how*?' Adam demanded. 'How is that even possible?'

A small smile crept across Harry's lips as he walked towards the edge of the room, where a huge drape was concealing something the size of a large van.

'I suppose *these* could come in handy.'

Harry whipped the drape away to reveal a mountain of boxes, all spilling over with silver cups.

'We were supposed to be using these for the InterNAL, but I think this might be more important.'

'NO WAY!' cheered Callum.

'Whoa!' gasped Adam.

'First thing tomorrow morning, we take your memory stick into the heart of the city, connect *all* of these cups to it, and get every single person in Derry to share a few hundred facts each, and it might just be enough to wake Popularis up.'

'YES!' Callum whooped with amazement as he dropped to his knees.

'Harry, you're a genius!' Adam laughed, clutching his face in disbelief.

'There's just one catch,' Harry announced, lowering his head as he delivered the bad news. 'People around here aren't big on social gatherings. Or talking. Ever. So … we're going to have our work cut out getting just one person to agree to come along.'

'We can do it!' Callum insisted. 'We'll get them there!'

'We're YouTubers, Harry!' Adam reminded him. 'Getting millions of followers is what we do best!'

'I hope so,' said Harry. 'Because you've only got twenty-two hours to get it done.'

'Twenty-two?' asked Callum. 'Why twenty-two?'

'Two reasons,' said Harry. 'First of all, by my calculations your phone battery will not last beyond that, even if you keep it powered off until the very last minute. Secondly, when I don't turn up to deliver the phone to those corrupt scientists tomorrow morning, they're going to do everything in their power to *take* it from us, so you two need to be gone before that happens.'

Adam tried to ignore the sudden dryness in his throat. Tried to ignore the panic that prickled every pore of his body. Tried to ignore the thought that was echoing through his brain –

This is the biggest, most difficult YouTube challenge of my life!

Callum must have seen the look of worry on his face, because he gently reminded him – 'B-Boys, Adam! We can do this! YouTubers, remember?'

Adam forced a smile. 'Yeah, Cal. YouTubers.'

Harry sighed in awe. 'Ahh, the power of music.'

13

Harry Is Our *Uncle*?!

Adam and Callum left Harry to his not-so-small job of connecting thousands of tin cups to a single USB cable, and headed back to Ethan's so they could begin their preparations to entice everyone in Derry to gather in the city centre the very next morning. On the bus, Adam stood alone in his cubicle, gawping at the advert on the wall and looking like a zombie who'd had a particularly bad night's sleep.

Callum was muttering something to him from his own cubicle, opposite, on the other side of the gangway, but Adam wasn't paying much attention to him.

'OK, let me get this straight,' Callum was

whispering, 'we've only got twenty-two hours to gather an entire city of people together, so that they can get us home by talking into a few thousand tin cans, except … none of these people actually *like* talking … or gathering … soooo, the first thing we do is jump on a bus and head to Ethan's shed? I don't want you to think I'm being critical, but that sounds like the worst plan you've ever come up with!'

Adam said nothing. He just stood there and continued to gawp at the ad.

'Hello? Earth to Adam? Are you ever going to stop staring at that advert? What does it even say? Free cake to whoever can pull the most gormless expression at this advert? Hey, are you OK?'

Adam finally tore his eyes away to see that Callum was no longer talking to him. He was poking his head into the cubicle next to him, where a little old man was quietly crying, by himself.

'Callum!' Adam hissed. 'You'll get us arrested!'

But this time it was Adam's turn to be ignored. He watched as Callum stepped into the cubicle and gently placed a hand on the man's shoulder. Adam couldn't hear what the old man was saying, only Callum's soft responses.

'It's fine! Rules were made to be broken, right? … Oh, no … That's really sad news. I'm sorry to hear that … Well, no, she probably *wouldn't* want you to be sad forever, but I guess you can't really tell your emotions what to do, can you? … I guess it's a bit like this scar on my knee – the cut stopped bleeding after a while, and then the scab eventually went away, but the scar is going to be there forever … Of course I'm wise! I'm a *genius* … Well, I'm glad it helped. Maybe you should do it more often! Like my mum always says – a problem shared is a problem halved … I know, I told you – genius … OK, well, I gotta go, but you take care now, OK?'

'What was *that* all about?' Adam whispered at Callum as he made his way back into his own cubicle.

'What was *this* all about?' Callum replied, mimicking Adam staring, slack-jawed and googly-eyed, at the advert on the cubicle wall.

Then Callum saw what it was that had got Adam so distracted.

'These adverts …' he gasped. 'They're supplied by BusScribers Advertising! That's Mum's business! I mean – alti-Mum – that's where she works!'

'And are you thinking what I'm thinking?' Adam whispered back.

'Err … well … I dunno.' Callum shrugged. 'I was mostly just thinking, you know, BusScribers, that's where alti-Mum works.'

Adam shook his head in disappointment. 'And I thought you were supposed to be a genius.'

The old man gave Callum a wave and a big smile through the window, as Adam and Callum disembarked at the bus stop nearest Ethan's house.

'So what am I missing?' Callum asked Adam, as he waved back at the old man. 'What's your big brainwave?'

'Don't you get it? Alti-Mum works in *advertising*! She gets messages out to hundreds of thousands of people, every day! And what do we need to do, right now?'

'Err … get lunch?'

'Callum, we need to tell the entire city to meet up in the city centre, first thing tomorrow morning! We don't have social media here! We can't just go online and send out a quick message on Instagram! Alti-Mum might be our only hope! If she can get some posters for us, and have them up on buses before everyone goes home from work at the end of the day, we might be able to spread the word!'

'Oh, right, yeah. Good idea. So, like, I guess we're getting back on a bus to go see alti-Mum then?'

'Yeah, except she'll be at work too, and I don't know where that is. It was written on that piece of headed paper, but we gave it to Harry. All I know is that it was somewhere on Stephington Lane, but that road was, like, five miles long! Ughhh, we don't have time for this! Now we're going to have to go all the way back to Harry's, to go all the way to

Mum's work, to come all the way back here!'

'No we don't,' said Callum. 'Miss E. Crawley, BusScribers Advertising, Floor 4, Lowers House, Stephington Lane, Derry.'

'What?' Adam laughed with disbelief. 'How on earth did you remember all of that?'

'Easy.' Callum shrugged. 'I'm a YouTuber!'

'OK, but that doesn't actually explain anything.'

'Yes it does. BusScribers Advertising – exactly the same as *subscribers* except "sub" is spelled backwards, then Floor 4, Lowers House – 4-Lowers – *followers*. See, easy. Told you I was a genius.'

'Yeah,' Adam muttered in reluctant agreement. 'I suppose you are. *Sometimes.*'

There was no one on reception at Lowers House, so Adam and Callum went straight up to floor 4, hoping to find an office with their mum's name on it – a job that turned out to be a lot easier than they had expected. Floor 4 only had five offices in total, and alti-Mum's office was the biggest, by far. Another thing they hadn't expected was who opened that office door when they knocked on it.

'HARRY?' Adam and Callum both gasped at the same time.

'Whoa! You do not waste any time, do you?' Callum laughed. 'You sly old goat!'

'How did you get here so quickly?' Adam puzzled. "I thought you had a few thousand wiring connections to make! You must have run out of the door the second we left!'

'I'm sure I have no idea what you're talking about,' Harry told them in a businesslike manner. 'I was merely passing by, and I thought I would return Miss Crawley's piece of paper to her.'

'Uh-huh, sure,' said Callum, stroking his chin.

'Of course you were,' Adam chuckled.

'Oh, hi! We were just talking about you two!' chirped alti-Mum as she appeared behind Harry to greet Adam and Callum. 'Harry was telling me all about your impromptu show you're putting on tomorrow. It's been such a long time since we've had a good concert. And we've *never* had one outside! And right in the city centre, too! It sounds so exciting! Don't worry, we've ordered posters, and they should be up and in the bus cubicles by this

237

afternoon. And all at a special discounted price. You know, *mates' rates*.'

'Are you serious?' said Adam, his mouth hanging open. 'That's … *amazing*! Thank you!'

'Not at all. Just as long as you save me a front-row seat at your concert. I've not seen much tuba music before, but I can't wait!'

'Our … *tuba* concert … yes!' said Adam, nodding slowly. 'Well, trust me, we're going to be *out of this world*!'

Leaving Harry to say his overly long goodbye to alti-Mum, Adam and Callum made their way towards the ground floor of Lowers House, and despite the good news about the free bus-cubicle posters, Callum had a look of worry on his face.

'That was a close call. She almost recognised us back there, Adam! Did you notice? And at Stephington, too! It's not going to be long until she figures out we're the two aliens who broke into her house and attacked her with a fake tree and a toilet brush! And then what? What if she calls the police on us again? It'll be kind of difficult to do our show from inside a police cell! It could ruin everything!'

'I know, Cal, but what can we do?' said Adam, looking just as worried. 'We're just going to have to avoid wearing PJs and carrying fake trees and toilet brushes whenever we're in her company, and hope for the best.'

At a jog, Harry caught up with them, which reminded Adam of *another* potential problem …

'*Tuba concert?*' Adam growled at Harry as he marched out of Lowers House and out on to Stephington Lane. 'TUBA CONCERT?'

'Really?' said Harry. 'That's all you have to say? Not "*Thank you, Harry, for spending your own hard-earned money on TWO THOUSAND posters on EXPRESS TURNAROUND!*"?'

'Thank you, Harry,' Adam sighed, 'even though you would probably have given up all your worldly possessions just for five minutes with *Miss Crawley*. But, still – *TUBA CONCERT?!*'

'Yes, Adam, a tuba concert – classical music, where nobody talks – something people around here *might* actually come to! What did you want on the posters, "*Come and enjoy a morning of talking into tin cups*"? Do you think that would have people turning up in their droves?'

'He has a point,' Callum told Adam.

'*I* have a point, too!' protested Adam. 'NEITHER OF US PLAYS THE TUBA!'

'I learnt the trumpet in school,' Callum reasoned. 'The tuba can't be *that* different. Plus, with these posters sorted, it means we can take the day off! Harry just needs to get all the tin cups ready for the morning, then we can, like, spend the day hanging out, before we have to … you know … *go*.'

'I … hate to break it to you, Callum, but those posters alone will get nowhere near enough people turning up tomorrow,' said Harry. 'They're just the tip of the iceberg. Only seven per cent of the city's population uses the buses, and only thirty-eight per cent of those actually pay any attention to the advertisements, and even then, we still don't know if any of those people will want to come along! Long story short – we still need as many hands on deck as possible to ensure that enough people turn up.'

'Oh,' said Callum, his shoulders drooping with

disappointment. 'So, no hanging out then? Just lots of hard work. Us doing our thing, you doing your thing, and then … that's it, we go home?'

'I'm afraid so,' said Harry, ruffling Callum's hair. 'The Beebop Boys aren't off the hook just yet.'

'It's just the B-Boys,' Adam corrected him.

'The Beat Boys?'

'*B*-Boys.'

'Oh, like the note, like B-sharp, or B-flat, or …'

'No, Harry, how many times do we have to explain this to you? We aren't in a band! We don't have anything to do with music! No bebop, no beats, no B-sharps. It's just B! You know, for *Beales*?'

'Ooh, that *would* be a good name for a band though, wouldn't it? The Beales!'

'Harry, we don't really have time for this,' Adam told him sternly. 'We now only have twenty-one hours to convince the entire population of Derry to gather in the city centre!'

'No, no, no, you have much less time than that!' Harry quickly corrected him. 'You have twenty-one hours until they have to *be* there. But if you think about it, they'll all be asleep for eight of those hours, and shut away in their homes for the whole evening, so that's another four or five hours, so, in actual fact, you've really only got until the end of the working day to be in with any chance of getting through to them, so, that's … what, five or six hours?'

'Oh dear,' Adam gulped. 'We better get to work!'

And that's exactly what they did. The brothers didn't waste a single second. They left Harry to get on with wiring up his thousands of tin cups, while they did what they do best – they made fools of themselves in public in hope of being 'viewed' as much as possible. But since they weren't exactly making videos for their usual audience, they knew it might take more than one attempt to find the winning altiverse approach …

Attempt No. 1 – Dustbin Lid Challenge

Knowing that they needed to drum up as much support as possible, Adam and Callum decided that's exactly what they'd try. *Literally*. Using big round metal dustbin lids as drums and wearing cardboard boxes as helmets, the brothers went on full military parade through the streets of Derry, banging their 'drums' and yelling their chant:

'Nine AM tomorrow!
In Guildhall Square!
The NAL revolution!
You better all be there!
The world is going to change
In ways to shout about
We'll explain it all tomorrow
If you miss it you'll miss out!'

It definitely got people's attention! But, when they heard the sound of police sirens heading their way, they wondered if maybe it was the *wrong* kind of attention. So they tried again …

Attempt No. 2 – Bus Challenge

This time, Adam and Callum went on a tour of the busiest bus stops in the city, hoping to get as many passengers as possible to notice their cubicle adverts. And they did this by singing (very badly) to the passengers as they waited for their buses, to the tune of 'Twinkle, Twinkle, Little Star'.

'When you take your bus today,
There is attention you must pay,
To Cubicle Adverts everywhere,
Read them all please talk and share,
The greatest show you ever will see,
The way you live is going to change, yippee,
Guildhall tomorrow, tell your chums,
It's the Nice and Lonely revolution!'

Some of the boarding passengers actually seemed to

warm to the idea of a song at a bus stop, and a few of them even seemed intrigued by how the NAL might be getting even better. But the bus drivers weren't quite so happy to see Adam and Callum pestering their customers, and one of them even got out of his cab and chased the pair down the street, yelling 'Talk and share? How dare you?! You can talk and share about my boot up your backsides if I ever catch you here again!'

'It's not working!' Adam panted, back in Harry's apartment.

'No one's listening!' added Callum.

'A bit like how *nobody* listened to me when I told them not to disturb me until I've finished wiring all of these tin cups,' Harry grumbled from somewhere inside a thicket of wires and cables in the middle of the room.

'I know you're busy, but we can't do this! We need help!'

'But you're the famous Beales Band!' Harry reminded them. 'This is what you do!'

'This is what we do using the *internet,* Harry!'

Adam reminded him. 'With social media and cameras and screens! The only screens you have here are *windows*, and we can't exactly ... Wait. Hang on! Maybe we *can*!'

'Can what?' asked Harry and Callum at the same time.

'We're going to need your gadgets and as much help as we can get,' said Adam. 'I think I know how we can do this.'

The first part of Adam's plan was the getting 'as much help as we can' bit, which involved trying to get Ethan and Bruce out of school. A plan that didn't go quite as smoothly as he'd hoped ...

'M-m-my rabbit's dead?' Ethan stammered, as a teacher brought him out of school so that 'Uncle Harry' could take him home.

'I'm so sorry, Ethan,' said the teacher. 'Apparently it choked on a lizard.'

'A l-l-*lizard*?' replied Ethan, looking confused and upset. 'And y-y-you're my *uncle*?' he gasped when he saw Harry. 'What's *going on*?'

'It's a confusing and upsetting time,' said Harry

as he thanked the teacher and put an arm around Ethan.

'I didn't even know I *had* a rabbit!' Ethan whimpered. 'That makes it even *more* sad!'

'You *don't* have a rabbit,' Adam whispered from behind a nearby hedge. 'I was hoping that might be a big enough clue for you to figure it out – we're getting you out of school early. We need your help!'

'Oh.' Ethan sighed with relief. 'Phew!'

'We need as much help as we can get, which is why you're not the only one we're springing from school today,' added Adam as out of the school doors came Bruce, also being consoled by a teacher, and looking even more confused and upset than Ethan.

'Are you absolutely *certain* we can trust him?' Adam asked Harry as he eyed Bruce with mounting uncertainty. 'I mean, his parents did just …'

'His parents are my friends who made a mistake with who they employed, that's all you can say against them right now,' Harry reminded Adam. 'And yes, like I told you before, I've known Bruce all his life, and I would trust him with my life.'

'Yeah,' growled Adam, 'but can we trust him with *our* lives? That's the question.'

'You aren't seriously still hung up on this whole "Bruce in our universe is evil" thing, are you?' Ethan asked in disbelief. 'Bruce has bent over backwards for you guys since the moment he met you, and you still don't trust him? If you ask me, he's not the one acting like a bad guy right now.'

Adam felt his stomach plummet with shame at the accuracy of Ethan's words.

'You're right,' he said. 'I'm being an idiot. Sorry.'

Adam felt sick with guilt for being so distrusting of Bruce, who really had been as good a friend as Ethan since they'd arrived in the altiverse. And overhearing the conversation between Bruce and the teacher only made Adam feel even worse –

'M-m-my *lizard* died?' he stammered with a wobbling bottom lip.

'I'm so sorry, Bruce,' said the teacher. 'Apparently it got eaten by a rabbit. But your uncle Harry is here to take you home.'

Harry thanked the teacher, and put an arm

around Bruce as the teacher disappeared back inside the school.

'You're my … *uncle?*' Bruce gasped at Harry.

'Mine too,' said Ethan with a shrug.

Then Bruce gave a yelp of surprise when he spotted Adam and Callum hiding behind a hedge.

'So … we're all *related?*'

Adam slapped a hand over his forehead.

'Considering you are two of the smartest people I've ever met, you're really not too bright.'

After apologising for upsetting them, then reassuring them that neither of them owned a rabbit or a lizard, and that no rabbits or lizards were harmed in the making of his lie, and that, no, Harry definitely *wasn't* secretly either of their uncles, Adam finally got around to explaining to Ethan and Bruce why he had got them out of school early.

'First thing tomorrow morning, we're gathering everyone in Derry to the city centre, and they're going to *talk*, which, with the help of science and Harry's overly large brain, will activate Callum's phone – his metal-and-glass *brick* – and send us back to our universe.'

Ethan and Bruce looked at each other, shrugged, then both said, 'That's cool.'

'And we need you two to help us get everyone to turn up,' Callum added.

'If you *want* to,' Harry interjected. 'Because there's something Adam needs to tell you.'

'Yeah.' Adam squirmed, struggling to make eye

contact with Bruce. 'We're kind of doing this against your parents' wishes. You see, they kind of have different plans for the phone, and they might be really annoyed if you help us.'

'Don't sweat it,' Bruce smiled, patting Adam on the back. 'They have quite a lot of plans that I choose to ignore. Just wait until they find out that I don't

want to help run Stephington Industries when I leave school; they're going to be mad at me for the rest of my life!'

'Thanks, Bruce,' said Adam, who was now feeling worse than ever, because even after all of this, he still couldn't bring himself to completely trust any son of Steph and Stan Kilter.

'So, what's the plan?' asked Ethan. 'How exactly are we going to get thousands of people to gather in the city centre tomorrow morning?'

'Well,' said Adam, 'basically, the four of us are going to be the first YouTube stars this altiverse has ever seen. How does that sound?'

Ethan and Bruce both looked at each other, then burst out laughing.

'It's never going to work, Adam! We've never played a tuba in our lives!'

Adam and Callum did not join in with the laughter.

'You know what?' Callum quietly growled to Adam. 'This whole "tuba" thing is starting to get really annoying.'

14

You Tubas Assemble

After returning to Harry's apartment, and promising not to bother him again until it was time to meet at Guildhall Square at 8.30 the next morning ready for the show, Adam and Callum, Ethan and Bruce each borrowed a tin-cup megaphone and two of his camera telescopia, then sprinted to the biggest office blocks they could find. It was all hands on deck. They found a clear, bright area to use as a 'stage', where they pointed one of the camera telescopia, then found the cleanest, whitest, shadiest side of a building and made sure that the back of the telescopia was facing that, and then it was time to see if it worked …

Adam and Callum stepped in front of the

telescopia, tin-cup megaphones in hand, and they gasped in amazement. The telescopia was projecting their images on to the side of the building, thirty feet tall, with crystal clarity, better and brighter than any projector they'd seen back home.

'OH MY WORD!' Adam cheered as he gazed up at the live display of the back of his head. 'This looks like we're broadcasting in UHD! It's even better than 8K! It's like IMAX on the side of a building!'

And then, remembering what they were there for, he spun around to face the front of the telescopia, raised the tin-cup megaphone to his mouth and slipped effortlessly into YouTube mode.

'Guys! Hello! My name is Adam B, this is my little bro, Callum B, and we are SO happy to be here!'

With his amplified voice echoing off every building, and the giant projection of his face on the wall behind him, it didn't take long before every office window had a worker's face in it, staring down at the show and wondering what on earth was going on.

'That's right!' added Callum, stepping forward. 'And together we … are … YOU TUBAS!'

Using a separate pair of tin-cup megaphones,

Ethan and Bruce added the biggest, most enthusiastic cheering and applauding they could muster, from off to the side, then Adam carried on.

'Tomorrow morning we will be putting on a show to remember! There will be live music! There will be tips on how to save loads of money each year on tissues – I mean *Tear-sues* – and Cuddle Gnomes! But most importantly, we will be unveiling something that will completely revolutionise the Nice and Lonely way of life! Something that will *totally* change the way you live! But you'll have to see it to believe it!'

'So please come along to join us!' said Callum. 'It's completely free of charge! Everyone's invited! Nine a.m., sharp! Guildhall Square! Be there or be … boring!'

'That's nine a.m.! Guildhall Square! Thank you! You've been great!' And then, without even realising it, Adam went into autopilot, and signed off exactly as he would on one of his YouTube videos – 'Guys! Smash that "Like" button and don't forget to press "Subscribe", and we'll see you bright and early tomorrow!'

A murmur of confusion cascaded down from the office windows, and Adam suddenly realised his mistake.

'Err ... forget that last bit. Don't actually smash anything. But we *will* see you bright and early tomorrow!'

They packed up their things and raced to the next street of office blocks, ready to do it all over again, except this time Adam handed the megaphones to Ethan and Bruce and told them, 'It's your turn, guys! I hope you were paying attention to how it was done!' Ethan and Bruce stared at him as if he'd just sneezed a canoe out of his nose.

'This is what I got you out of school for!' Adam laughed. 'We need to do this on every major street in the city! Me and Cal can't do it by ourselves! You two do the north side, we'll do the south side, and we'll meet in the middle when we're done, OK?'

Ethan and Bruce stared at Adam as if a little green alien had just climbed out of his bellybutton and asked them to clean its ears with their underpants.

'Can we, like, watch you do it one more time, first, please?' asked Ethan, who was gradually turning green with terror.

'Or maybe five or ten more times,' suggested Bruce, who was currently unable to move with fear.

Adam and Callum did two more little shows, then assured the two nervous wrecks that 'you've got this!' before sending them off to do their own versions.

'Do you really think we can trust Bruce?' asked Callum.

'If he's anything like his parents, Cal, I don't think we can trust him any further than we could catapult him with a teaspoon, but Ethan and Harry both say that we can trust him, and I *do* trust what they say.'

Ethan and Bruce's show wasn't quite as polished and professional as Adam and Callum's, and the whole idea of speaking in front of lots of people seemed like an entirely alien concept, but they did manage to remember all the key points, so that was something.

'Good afternoon,' said Ethan, looking at Bruce, and using an unusually posh and unnatural voice.

'Good afternoon to you too,' said Bruce, just as awkwardly. 'We are here because we … err … have come to be here.'

Uncomfortable pause.

'Yes,' said Ethan. 'That is right. And … erm … we would like to tell you, also, all of you, that also, tomorrow, there will also be a show.'

'Yes,' Bruce confirmed, looking like a nodding dog. 'That is correct. It will be a musical show. With … erm … music.'

'That is right,' said Ethan, standing as still as a plank of wood. 'It will also be informative. With moneysaving tips.'

'That is right,' added Bruce. 'And there will be some extremely amazing news and information on how our NAL way of life is about to be even more extremely and amazingly better than it already is.'

'That is right,' agreed Ethan. 'And it will be at Guildhall Square. At nine a.m. In the morning. And you should all come along for some entertainment and …'

'Information,' Bruce finished for him.

'Yes. That is right. Thank you, everybody. Smash my like and … err … push my subscribe? Goodbye.'

Adam and Callum winced at the awkwardness of their co-presenters.

'I think they might *put people off* coming rather than entice them!' Callum quietly muttered to Adam.

Adam was about to agree when, to his amazement, dozens of office windows opened up and the people inside began *applauding*.

'I don't get it!' Adam reeled in surprise. 'Nobody cheered *us*!'

'We thought we'd improve on what you did,' Ethan explained after he'd exited the 'show'. 'Don't get me wrong, you two did pretty well, but it was a bit too, you know, *loud* and *fast*.'

'Kind of messy,' added Bruce. 'Too much to take in all at once.'

'I guess the people in this altiverse like it slow and simple,' said Callum with a shrug.

'I guess so,' agreed Adam, numbly. 'I think we might need to alter our routine!'

So Adam and Callum left Ethan and Bruce to carry on slam-dunking one teaser show after another and then spent the rest of the afternoon desperately trying to match them – putting on the most robotic, unenthusiastic, emotionless teaser in front of as many office blocks as they could manage.

Hours later, when all the offices were closed, and everyone was shut away in their Nice and Lonely homes, Adam, Callum, Ethan and Bruce called it a day. Between them, they had put on thirty-eight teaser shows all over Derry, and despite their best efforts, Adam and Callum never managed to be quite as impressively awful as Ethan and Bruce.

'Guys, we can't thank you enough for all your help today,' Adam told them just as he and Callum were preparing to sneak back into Ethan's shed. 'You were *amazing*!'

Ethan brushed the compliment away with a swipe of his hand.

'Stop iiiiiiiit,' he giggled, blushing slightly.

'Seriously!' Adam insisted. 'You could do this kind of thing professionally – altiverse Creators – you could be *famous*!'

'Well, before you get zapped back home, maybe we'll give you some pointers,' suggested Ethan, 'and maybe one day, back in your universe, you might be as good at it as us!'

Adam had a funny feeling that Ethan was being deadly serious.

'Thanks,' Adam said with a smile. 'That'd be cool.'

'Except I'm not sure there'll be time,' said Callum, quickly checking the time on his phone. 'We've got to be up at the crack of dawn to meet Harry at Guildhall Square.'

'Good point,' said Bruce. 'See you there. Eight-thirty, right?'

'Eight-thirty,' Adam confirmed.

'I'll wake you guys before my parents get up, about seven a.m.,' Ethan told Adam and Callum. 'Then we can get an early bus to the city, so there's no chance of being late.'

Adam and Callum agreed on the plan, said their goodnights, thanked Ethan and Bruce again, then shut themselves in the shed and got into their sleeping bags for the last time.

'I'm actually going to miss this place,' Adam

mused as he stared at the shed ceiling.

'I'm going to miss Dad,' Callum said solemnly. 'I'm really going to miss him, Adam.'

'I know, Cal. Me too. It sucks that we have to go, but we really do have to.'

'I know. It's just … If only I'd charged my phone that morning before I left the house. Imagine if it had been at one hundred per cent when we got here … even just fifty per cent. Think about it: a measly ten per cent could have meant one more day with Dad.'

'Hey, Cal, I'm almost afraid to ask, but when you looked at your phone …?'

'Seven per cent,' said Callum, second-guessing what Adam was going to ask.

'Only seven per cent?!' gasped Adam. 'Oh man. Keep it turned off, Cal. We mustn't turn it back on until we use it to get back home.'

'*If* we get back home,' Callum corrected him. 'I wonder how Dad – I mean – how Harry's getting on with all of those tin cups.'

'Poor guy's probably going to be at it all night,' Adam groaned, feeling guilty that they weren't skilled enough to be able to help him.

'What about us – what we did. Do you think it worked? Do you think enough people will turn up tomorrow?'

'I guess we'll find out,' said Adam.

And eight seconds later Callum was snoring.

Adam was just moments away from drifting off himself, when a noise from Ethan's garden snapped him wide awake again. He froze, listening intently, hoping to hear Ethan's voice bidding them 'good-night'. But no 'goodnight' came, just the sound of rustling leaves in the hedge next to the shed. Adam knew that it was probably just a cat or a hedgehog, but remembering the hungry looks on the faces of all those dodgy scientists that morning, Adam began to imagine them all, hiding outside, in the dark, waiting to sneak in and steal the phone. Silently, Adam sat up in his sleeping bag and locked the shed door from the inside, just to be safe.

A little later on there were more noises outside the shed, but Adam was already falling asleep, and his brain incorporated the sounds into his dream, a dream that he was in his bed, and the sounds he could hear were coming from Mum clattering around in the kitchen. Adam's restful face smiled, and he murmured in his sleep – 'Don't worry, Mum. Nearly home. Just one more night. Promise.'

15

Butterfingers, Jelly and a Very Big Oven

Shock kicked in like a punch to the face.

'Callum?' Adam whispered as he stared in panic at Callum's empty sleeping bag.

It was barely even light outside. Probably 6.30 a.m. Callum *never* got up this early. *Never!*

'Callum!' Adam whispered even louder, whipping Callum's sleeping bag away, hoping to find that he had simply climbed out of his sleeping bag in his sleep and rolled off the airbed on to the shed floor.

No such luck. Callum was gone. His clothes were gone. His phone was gone. And the shed door was unlocked.

Adam felt sick with worry.

Has something happened to him?

Is there an emergency that I don't know about?

Is Harry OK?

Is it later than I think, and everyone's waiting for me at Guildhall Square?

Has Callum gone there early, just to get a little extra time with him before we leave?

Or is he hiding, so we NEVER have to leave?

Has he gone for a secret meeting with Stan and Steph and their dodgy scientists?

Or ... has he just gone outside for a quick hedge wee?

Adam's heart rate dropped by eight million beats per minute as he realised that this was by far the most likely possibility, and he felt like a bit of an idiot for not considering it first. He leant over to push the shed door open, almost certain that he'd see Callum standing next to the hedge, pretending to chop it to pieces with his pee-coloured light-sabre, but then he spotted it – wedged in the jamb of the shed door was a piece of folded paper. A note. And when Adam read it, his heart almost stopped.

> Adam!
> The Kilters have found a way to charge the battery using the Boiler Room at Stephington Industries! Thought I'd give it a go. Don't be mad!
> Callum

'No!'

Adam threw his clothes on.

'No, no, no!'

He raced out of Ethan's garden.

'Callum, you idiot!'

He sprinted to the bus stop.

'They'll destroy the phone!'

There was a bus already waiting, and he jumped straight on.

'They'll run the battery down!' he growled, puncturing the silence of the bus.

He stared at the cubicle poster for his own show –

Tuba concert to reveal the new NAL revolution! Guildhall Square, 9 a.m.

'We're going to miss our own show!' he moaned as he bounced up and down on the balls of his feet, willing the bus to go faster.

'C'mon! *C'mon!*'

After what felt like an eternity, the bus finally arrived on Stephington Lane. Adam shot from the bus and rocketed into Stephington Industries.

'Please don't let me be too late! *Please* don't let me be too late!'

The reception was empty except for a lone security guard standing beneath the clock – 7.20 a.m.

'No! He could have been here for an hour already!'

Adam bolted down the stairs.

'Boiler Room! Boiler Room!'

But when he got to the basement, he couldn't find anywhere that looked like it could be a boiler room. It was filled with the fanciest, top of the range executive offices, and then Adam realised –

'This is the altiverse, you idiot! They love privacy! Of course all the best offices are in the basement! So the boiler room must be in the place that has the biggest views across the whole city – the roof!'

So, with tired and trembling legs, Adam went bounding back up the stairs, two at a time, until he reached the very top.

'Nearly there,' he panted. 'Nearly there.'

He emerged from a door and was almost blinded by the reflection of the rising sun off the aluminium roof that stretched out before him. Shielding his eyes, he stepped out onto a steel mesh walkway and instantly saw a shed-type building a short distance off to his right. Adam didn't need to read the sign on the door to know what this was –

'The Boiler Room!'

Adam darted over to it, threw the door open, then ground to a halt.

The room was completely black, and Adam couldn't figure out why this wasn't the most sought-after office space of them all – completely cut off from the rest of the building, not a single window, it was possible the most secluded and lonely place in the entire *city*. Adam reached in and flipped the light switch, which made no difference whatsoever.

'Broken,' Adam hissed under his breath. 'Great.'

Then, stepping into the darkness, Adam called out – 'Callum? Hello?'

But the only reply he got was the metallic echo of his voice bouncing back at himself. Going from the blinding roof to the blackness of the boiler room was a jarring contrast, and Adam's eyes hadn't adjusted to the dark yet, but so far there seemed to be no sign of Callum. No scientists. No *anybody*.

'CALLUM!' he called again.

Still no response.

And then he saw it! Over in a corner – a glowing light! Adam fumbled his way across to it, bashing his head and shins on various pipes and cabinets along the way, and he gave a gasp of shock and relief when he saw where the light was coming from –

'Callum's phone!'

It didn't make sense. If Callum's phone was there, then where was Callum? For days, everyone at Stephington Industries had treated this phone like it was a Diamond Play Button, so why was it now just left discarded in the Boiler Room?

Adam's head was spinning. He looked around at the room, hoping to see some trace of Callum, but the light of the phone shining in his eyes only made the rest of the room seem even darker.

Adam looked down at the screen to see if it had enough battery for him to risk using the phone's torch, and was surprised to find a yellow sticky note stuck to the screen, illuminated from behind, making it easy to read what was written on it –

Adam! Turn on the phone! You won't believe what happens next!

Adam pulled the note from the screen, gave a gasp of horror to see that the battery was only at five per cent, then gave another gasp of horror as something that felt like a spider tickled the back of his neck. He gave a few frantic swipes at his neck, then punched in Callum's four-digit security pin, activating the phone.

The note was not wrong – Adam really *didn't* believe what happened next. The phone was snatched from his hand. The lights came on, dazzling him, and he turned to see that he hadn't been alone at all. He was completely surrounded by the dozen dodgy scientists, Callum had his arms tied around a thick metal pipe, just six feet away, and directly behind him was Mrs Kilter, her hands clasped tightly around Callum's nose and mouth, so that he couldn't make a sound. And finally, behind him, was Mr Kilter, so close that Adam could count the number of hairs curling out of his nostrils. The spider he'd felt hadn't been a spider at all, it had been Mr Kilter's breath on the back of his neck, watching as he unlocked Callum's phone.

'Thank you for that,' said Mr Kilter smoothly and politely as he waved Callum's phone in front of Adam. 'We'd spent a long time trying to make Callum tell us that code, and then you go and show it to us in less than a minute. Now that you've unlocked it for us, we can finally get to work, taking it to pieces, figuring out how it's made, so that we can reproduce it ourselves and sell each one for a small fortune. Think about it, Adam, these devices make the InterNAL look like something from the Stone Age! We can completely revolutionise the NAL way of life, and get *very* rich in the process.'

'Yeah?' said Adam. 'Well, *we've* got a NAL revolution of our own, and you're going to make us late, so if you don't mind …'

Adam lunged for the phone in Mr Kilter's hand, but Mr Kilter leaped back as four of the scientists pounced on Adam, marched him over to Callum and cuffed his hands around the metal pipe with thick black cable ties.

'I'm afraid your little show will have to be cancelled,' Mrs Kilter purred with glee, 'since its two main stars will shortly be dead.'

She stepped over to another set of pipes, which had a big, red, wheel-shaped tap attached to it, and she began to turn.

'In about three minutes, this boiler room will heat up to a minimum temperature of ninety degrees Celsius, and you two will be cooked alive, like a pair of boiled maggots.'

'You can't do that!' Callum roared. 'It's MURDER!'

'Oh, Callum, I'm not going to murder *anybody*,' Mrs Kilter assured him with a serpentine smile. 'You see, in order to be murdered, you need to *exist* in the first place. And in this universe, you have no birth certificates, no family, no home, and the only credible adult who could vouch for your existence – a certain Harry Beales – will shortly be classified as insane by twelve of the country's top scientists. So how could I be murdering anybody, when you two are quite literally *nobodies*? We can do anything we like, and not even get in any trouble for it.'

Adam and Callum both screamed and yelled in protest, but Mr and Mrs Kilter acted as if they couldn't hear a thing as they casually strolled out of the room, handing the phone to Professor Arty-Facće.

'I trust you *can* recharge this battery, Professor Arty-Facće?' said Mrs Kilter, handing him the phone.

'My eels vill have it in tip-top condition in two shakes of a lamby-vammy's tail,' Professor Arty-Facće assured her.

And then the door closed, plunging Adam and Callum into inky darkness.

Adam twisted and pulled at the cable tie around his wrists, determined to break free, but it was no use. The only thing at risk of breaking was his skin.

'Adam?' Callum's trembling voice quaked. 'I'm sorry.'

'I don't get it, Cal,' Adam growled through gritted teeth. 'Why did you come here? We had a plan! It could have worked!'

'I … Adam, you think I *came* here?! No! They *kidnapped* me! I left the shed to do a hedge wee, and they were right there – Mrs and Mrs Kilter – in Ethan's garden! Before I knew it, they had me tied up and in the back of a van!'

'What? Are you OK?' gasped Adam.

'I'm fine. Well, my wrists are a bit sore, but hey.'

'I still don't get it though. You left a note!'

'No! Are you kidding me? Do you not even know what my handwriting looks like? *I* didn't write that note, *they* did! As soon as they figured out that the phone had a screen lock, and that I wasn't going to give them the security code, they came back and planted that note! A trap! To trick you into putting the code in, right in front of them!'

Adam gave a deep sigh as he rested his forehead against the pipe.

'I'm such an idiot.'

'No you're *not*, you're a *hero*! You came to rescue me!'

'Cal, of course I came to rescue you!' Adam said with a snort of laughter. 'You're my *little brother*!'

'I'm sorry I got us into this, Adam.'

'Cal, it's not your fault. Like you said, they *kidnapped* you!'

'No, I mean this *whole situation*. We'd be safe, back home, with Mum, if I had only listened to you, and stopped messing with Popularis, trying to find out more about Dad.'

Adam wished that there was just a shred of light to see by, because he desperately wanted to look in Callum's eyes as he spoke, but it was so dark that there was no difference between having his own eyes open or closed. So he made do with *picturing* Callum's eyes instead.

'Cal, thanks to you, we've just had the biggest adventure of our lives. Of *anybody's* lives! We found an ALTERNATE UNIVERSE! It's the greatest discovery of all time! And we *did* get to spend time with Harry, and that was just the BEST. Cal, if I could change one thing about this week, I would change *me*. I'd go back and listen to you more. You've been saying it all week – I treat you like your ideas don't matter. And they *do* matter. They matter just as much as mine, because we're a team, Cal. We're the B-Boys!'

'Thanks,' Callum said softly. 'Adam? It's getting *really* hot in here.'

'Yeah, I noticed. It's literally like an oven.'

Adam was the hottest he'd ever been in his life. Sweat was pouring into his eyes, his T-shirt was soaked from top to bottom, and the air was so hot and dry, every breath felt like he was inhaling flames.

'Adam?' Callum's voice trembled. 'What are we going to do? That science idiot is going to destroy our phone!'

'Callum, they're going to destroy *us*!'

'But … they won't really. Not when you've broken free.'

Adam gave another sigh as he let his arms slide down the pipe, and he sat on the floor.

'Cal, I'm sorry. I've tried, but it's *impossible*. They've cuffed us with eight-millimetre cable ties!

We'd need arms the size of tree trunks to break through these things!'

'Nuh-uh, not tree trunks, just arms as big as your legs,' Callum corrected him, his voice bouncing with positivity.

'I don't have arms as big as my legs either, Callum!' Adam groaned in exasperation. 'In case you hadn't noticed, my arms are exactly *arm-sized*!'

And then, to Adam's utter disbelief, Callum actually started *laughing*.

'B-Boys video number forty-three, Adam, don't you remember? "Adam's Great Escapes"! First, I tied your hands and feet together with ropes, and you showed how to break free. Then I locked you in the garage, and you showed how to break free. And then …'

'You tied me to a chair with eight-millimetre cable ties!' Adam cheered as the memory of the video came flooding back to him.

'And you … well, you didn't break free from that one because apparently I'd pulled the cable ties too tight, but …'

'But I remember what I need to do, and, Cal …'

Adam jumped back to his feet, and wriggled his arms back and forth.

'These cable ties aren't too tight! I think I can do it!'

Adam had just enough wiggle room to reach his right hand across to undo his belt. He slid the belt from his jeans, carefully fed it through the loop of the cable tie around his wrist, then fastened the belt back up. Now all he needed to do was put his foot into the loop of the belt, pull up with his hands and push down with his foot, using all his strength. Adam's leg muscles trembled under the strain, he pushed and he pulled and then … the heat became too much for him to bear. Blood rushed to his head, the room began to spin, and Adam slumped against the pipe, only half-conscious.

'Adam, what happened?' Callum cried out. 'Did you do it?!'

Adam could only groan in reply.

'Adam, what's wrong?!'

'Too hot,' Adam managed to mutter. 'I don't have the strength.'

There was a hollow CLANG as Adam lost consciousness and his head hit the pipe.

'Adam? You OK?' asked Callum.

Adam could just about hear him, but Callum sounded a long way away, as if he was hearing him from inside a dream.

'ADAM! Listen to me! You have to stay awake, OK? We can do this! We can do it together! I'll help!'

Callum reached around the pipe, found Adam's hands and clung on to his wrists. Then he hooked his leg around, finding Adam's belt, and slipped his foot inside it, next to Adam's.

Adam felt his little brother holding his hands, and it sent a surge of defiance through Adam's body. He took a deep breath, then straightened himself out.

'YES, ADAM! YES!'

'We can do this, Cal,' Adam whispered.

'YES!'

'B-Boys, Cal!'

'B-BOYS!'

'In three ... two ... ONE!'

Both brothers pulled with their hands, pushed

with their feet. Blood rushed to both their heads, the whole world went fuzzy, and then it happened –

SNAP! The cable tie broke! Adam was free! He stumbled back and fell to the floor. His hand hit a spanner, and he grabbed it tight in his grasp, then clambered to his feet, slid the spanner between Callum's cable tie and the pipe, then let his own weight do the hard work, pulling down on the spanner, like a lever, until Callum's cable tie snapped too.

'YES!' they both cheered at the same time, before scrambling through the darkness towards the tiniest sliver of light that crept in through the hinges of the door.

The two of them burst out into the dazzling daylight, drinking in the fresh air as if it were ice-cold spring water. They gave themselves ten seconds to recover, to cool down, to revel in the glory of not being cooked alive, and then they got to their feet and ran. Neither of them spoke, because they didn't need to, they both seemed to know exactly where they were headed – the lab where they first met the twelve dodgy scientists. Adam just hoped they weren't too late – every second they spent running could be the exact second that Professor Arty-Facće plopped Callum's phone into a watery tank of electric eels.

They raced down stairs, they weaved through crowds of office workers, they burst through doorways, and then they were there, directly outside the doors to the lab. Callum was about to barge straight in when Adam put out a hand to stop him. He held a finger to his lips – *shhh* – and then, slowly, they pushed the door open, and silently crept in.

There they were, all twelve scientists, all with their backs to the door as they gathered around one bench, on which sat a huge fish tank that was filled so densely with electric eels that there was barely any room for the water. And right in the centre of the twelve scientists was Professor Arty-Facće, with a wooden pole in one hand, which he was using to agitate the eels in the tank, and in the other hand, gripped tightly, was Callum's phone, bone dry, and yet to take the plunge.

'That's it, my little eely-veelies, get as excited as possible, because I vant every last spark of electricity from you! Yes, yes, I know, you vant your

284

fishy-vishy food, and you vill get it in just one minute, and after zat I vill feed you a phone, vhich you will recharge until the batteriez are at full capacity, iz zat understood?'

Adam spotted the large plastic tub of fish food on the workbench, next to Professor Arty-Facće, then he noticed the shelves full of chemicals and ingredients directly behind himself and Callum, and an ingenious idea flashed through his brain.

'Callum,' he whispered, 'I've got a plan.'

'We beat them down with our kung-fu skills?'

'That *could* be a plan,' Adam mused, 'except you seem to be forgetting two tiny little details. Number one, there are *twelve* of them. And number two, we don't have any kung-fu skills.'

'We could make it up as we go along,' Callum suggested with a shrug. 'How hard can it be?'

'Callum, there's no way we're going to be able to wrestle that phone from twelve scientists. Our only hope of getting it is once Professor Farty Face has let go of it.'

'Adam!' Callum hissed. 'He's not going to let go of it until he throws it into the tank of water!'

285

'That's the idea,' Adam whispered with a wink. 'We're going to beat them with *science*.'

Adam spun around and began searching the shelves for one specific ingredient.

'What are you doing?' Callum hissed. 'My phone is going to drown any minute now!'

'B-Boys video number twenty-six, don't you remember?' Adam told him with a cheeky smile. 'We're looking for something called Sodium Poly-something-or-other. Help me look.'

The chemicals were all stored alphabetically, so it wasn't long before Callum pulled a jar off the shelf labelled 'Sodium Polyacrylate' and asked – 'Is this it?'

Adam gave him a thumbs up and a big grin, before quietly taking all six jars of the stuff off the shelf, then dumping their contents into a plastic tub identical to the one Professor Arty-Faccé had with the fish food in. With the scientists happily distracted by the eels and the phone, Adam led the way, tiptoeing around the outer edge of the room until he reached the end of the long workbench and, without being spotted by a single scientist, he and Callum climbed underneath the bench, and crawled down to the centre until they were directly beneath the fish tank full of eels, and surrounded by twenty-four scientist-legs. Without wasting a second, Adam swiftly and quietly reached up, snatched the tub of fish food away, and seamlessly replaced it with the tub of sodium polyacrylate.

'I don't remember B-Boys video number twenty-six!' Callum whispered. 'What is that stuff?'

'You don't remember? Cal, it's the powder they put inside babies' nappies!'

Professor Arty-Faćće cleared his throat.

'And now zat ze eels are full of energy, I vill vhip them into a frenzy by adding a whole tub of fish food, and zen ve vill drop in ze battery-powered device!'

Adam heard the *SLOOSH* of the powder being tipped into the water, followed by the *SPLASH* of the eels churning feverishly through the water, and finally came the sound of the phone being dropped in. But instead of making the 'PLOP' sound that everyone had expected, it made a loud 'SLAP' as, rather than sinking *into* the water, it landed *on top* of it!

'VHAT IZ GOING ON HERE!' wailed Professor Arty-Facćé as he stared down at the tank, which was now filled with a thick, slushy gel.

'Jellied eels,' Adam explained as he popped up from beneath the workbench and swiped the phone from the top of the tank. 'Thank you!'

Ducking back down, Adam and Callum leaped through the gaps between the scientists' legs, and dashed for the door.

'STOP ZOSE PESKY LITTLE KIDDIE-VINKS!' yelled Professor Arty-Facćé as he and the other eleven scientists raced after the Beales boys.

'I remember it now!' Callum cheered as they burst through the doors of the lab and out into the corridor. 'B-Boys video number twenty-six – "How to Make Slime from Babies' Nappies"!'

But their moment of triumph came to an abrupt halt when, on the other side of the lab door, they came face-to-face with Mr and Mrs Kilter, waiting for them with outstretched arms.

'AHAAAA!' roared the Kilters.

'AAAAAAARGHHHHHHH!' roared the Beales boys.

SLAM went their bodies as the four of them collided.

'OOOOF!' they exhaled in unison as they all hit the floor.

Then – 'Ooooh, ouch, ah!' groaned the Kilters as they painfully got back to their feet, and …

'Catcha later!' called Adam as he and Callum effortlessly sprang back to their feet and carried on down the corridor, pursued by the twelve scientists.

Adam couldn't help it – a triumphant laugh burst from his mouth as he began racing up the stairs. But his laugh died in the air as he glanced over his shoulder to see that Stan and Steph Kilter had caught back up with them! They were at the front of the pack of scientists and just a hair's breadth behind Adam! Adam did his best to speed up, but he had simply done too much running for one day and, rather than going faster, his legs were slowing down. Steph Kilter's fingertips were clutching at his shoulder! Panic was coursing through his veins!

Callum was up on the ground floor, racing towards the doors. Adam still had half a flight of stairs to go, and Stan was now directly beside him, reaching for the phone in Adam's hand.

I'm not going to make it! Adam thought. *I'm too tired!*

He reached the ground floor. He launched himself towards the doors. Two pairs of Kilter hands had a firm grasp of his arms. He couldn't run!

They pulled him back! And then –

SLAM!

Someone collided with the Kilters.

Someone gave a wail of surprise.

Arms and limbs were everywhere as Stan and Steph went crashing to the floor in a storm of fluttering papers and the scientists went tumbling over the top of them in a twelve-scientist pile-up.

Adam was free! He ran to the doors and looked back to see alti-Mum scrabbling to pick up the hundreds of pieces of paper that Stan, Steph and the scientists were slipping around in. It happened very briefly, in little more than a second, but Adam didn't miss it – alti-Mum turned his way, gave a smile and a wink, then mouthed – 'GO!'

As Adam and Callum raced for the bus, proud

smiles spread across their faces as they heard alti-Mum behind them.

'Oh dear me, I *am* sorry! Please let me help you up. Oh, butterfingers! Let's try that again. Oopsie-daisy! I seem to be making it *worse*! How about if I ... Oh dear, silly me ...'

And as their bus pulled away, they chuckled with glee to see fourteen fools still floundering in a fountain of paperwork.

16

Goodbye

The bus stopped just around the corner from Guildhall Square, which was lucky for Adam because his morning had been filled with so much running, so much adrenalin and so much almost-being-cooked-alive, that his legs now felt as though they were made of jelly.

'It's 8.57,' said Callum, peering up at the clock atop the Guildhall tower. 'We made it!'

Seeing Callum use an actual clock to tell the time, rather than his phone, reminded Adam that he still had Callum's phone in his pocket, and that he hadn't checked to make sure that the Kilters hadn't damaged it when they stole it. To his relief, the phone looked fit and well, but it wasn't all good news …

'No!' Adam blurted. 'Cal! We've only got three per cent battery!'

Callum turned as white as a sheet.

'Adam, turn it off! Turn it off! That thing sometimes shuts down on me when it says it's still got *ten* per cent! It could go at any minute!'

Adam powered it off, then the two exhausted brothers hurried, as best they could, towards Guildhall Square, but came to an abrupt halt when a shadowy figure emerged from the back of a nearby van, stepping directly in front of them.

'AAAAAAAARRRGHHHHHH!' Adam and Callum both screamed.

Adam clutched the phone for dear life.

Callum jumped into made-up kung-fu mode, ready to attack.

And the figure in front of them let out a high-pitched shriek as he dropped the armful of cables he'd been carrying.

'HARRY!' Adam gasped with relief as both he and Callum threw their arms around their alti-dad. 'You scared the life out of us!'

'You scared the life out of *me*!' Harry retorted,

not quite knowing how to hug something that wasn't a Cuddle Gnome, and ending up patting the two boys' heads. 'I was worried you weren't going to turn up! You were supposed to be here half an hour ago!'

'Well, we're here now,' said Adam, stepping back from the non-hug to catch his breath. 'And so are *you*, thank goodness!'

'Of course I'm here. I've been here *all night*. Where else would I be?'

'I was worried that the Kilters might have got to you!' Adam explained.

'Got to me?' Harry blustered with a confused laugh. 'The *Kilters*? Boys, boys, I've told you before, yes, the Kilters can seem a little strange from time to time, but trust me, they would never ...'

'They *kidnapped us!*' Callum interjected. 'They stole my phone! They locked us in the Boiler Room! They TRIED TO KILL US!'

Harry staggered backwards. He looked like he'd been hit around the head with a sack of jellied eels. And he was completely lost for words.

'They ... in ... and ... then ... are you *sure*?!'

'They tried to kill us, Harry,' Adam firmly assured him. 'It was kind of hard to miss. And they're probably still after us. They could be arriving on the very next bus for all we know, so we need to get home *fast*, before they catch up with us.'

'They actually stole your phone?' Harry muttered, staring off into nowhere while his brain struggled to keep up with this news.

'Yes,' said Adam.

'The *Kilters*?'

'Yes,' said Adam.

'And they *kidnapped* you?'

'Yes,' said Adam.

'Stan and Steph?'

'Yes,' said Adam.

'And they tried to *kill* you?'

'Yes,' said Adam.

'And this is in *real life*? In *this* universe?'

'Yes,' said Adam.

'How could I have been so wrong about them?'

'I don't know,' said Adam.

'They were my *friends*.'

'I know,' said Adam.

'How could they do this?'

'I don't know,' said Adam.

'I *trusted* them!'

'I know,' said Adam.

'They ...'

'They're bad guys, OK?' Callum said urgently, his lip wobbling. 'They made you think they were nice when actually they're not, because that's what bad guys do. Now *please* can we focus on the whole "getting us home" thing, because we probably don't have long until the *bad guys* catch up with us and ruin *everything*. Or should we just stand around here gawping like a bunch of bananas for a few more minutes?'

'You're right, Callum,' said Harry, snapping himself out of his stupor. 'We need to focus.'

'Good. Right. So, did you get all the tin cups finished?' asked Callum as he and Adam began marching towards the square while Harry scooped up his cables, and huffed and puffed behind.

'Well, yes, but ...'

'Great! How many are there?' asked Adam. 'Enough to get us home?'

'Well, yes, but …'

'How many people turned up?' Callum wanted to know. 'Hundreds? Thousands? *Millions?* There are people there, aren't there?'

'Well, yes, but …'

'Please stop saying "but" like that!' Adam gently pleaded. 'You're making it sound like something's gone wrong, and it's making me nervous! What is it, Harry? "But" *what?*'

'Welllllll …'

The trio rounded the corner, on to Guildhall Square, and Harry's 'but' was plain to see …

Adam and Callum stopped dead in their tracks, and now it was *their* turn to stumble backwards in shock, *their* turn to look like they'd been hit around the heads with a sack of jellied eels, *their* turn to be completely lost for words.

The tin cups were there, all over Guildhall Square and the streets beyond, thousands upon thousands of the things, each atop a pole, like a short microphone stand, in neat, uniform rows. But Adam's heart sank straight down to his stomach, and his stomach sank straight down to his feet, when he saw that there were *not* millions of people there. Not thousands. Not even *hundreds*. Instead, there was a grand total of ... *two*. Ethan and Bruce, who were helping to add the finishing touches to the stage.

After a great effort, Adam finally managed to force words out of his mouth.

'H-H-H-Harry ... w-where is everyone?'

Ethan was placing a glitter cannon at the back of the stage, which had been constructed at the top of the hall steps, directly outside the grand doors. Bruce was busy up a ladder, attaching an extra light to the scaffold rig, which made an arc over the front of the stage. And each and every minuscule noise they made echoed out across the silent and empty Guildhall Square.

'Well ...' Harry began, his face twisted in a pained grimace. 'It's only five past nine, so there's still plenty of time for people to ...'

'And why is *Bruce* here!' Callum interrupted, his eyes narrowed with distrust.

'Bruce and Ethan came as soon as they realised that you weren't in the shed,' Harry explained, sounding like a parent for the first time since they'd met him, with a 'now, you listen here …' tone to his voice. 'They assumed you must have come here early. They've *both* been worried sick about you, and they have *both* been working their socks off to help get this finished for you. So, regardless of what Stan and Steph might have done, you cannot tarnish Bruce with the same brush, understood?'

'Understood,' Adam agreed abashedly.

Harry busied himself with his armful of cables, plugging them into various connectors at the side of the stage, while Callum gave Adam a sharp elbow to the ribs.

'*Understood?* Are you serious?'

'Of course I'm not serious, Cal! All right, yes, Bruce has been acting like a totally decent guy this whole time, but what if that's just so he can pass insider information back to his parents about us, about your phone? We can't be too careful. We have to keep a very close eye on him. But at the same time, we can't let him know that we suspect him. If he thinks we trust him, then he'll keep his guard down, and that'll make it easier for us to catch him in the act if he's trying to help his parents get to us. Does that make sense?'

'Kiiinnnd of,' said Callum, his mouth all askew with confusion.

'Basically, if he *is* working against us, he'll be a lot sneakier about it if he knows we're watching him, and we don't like sneaky, we want to be able to spot if he's up to something. Got it?'

'Got it.'

'Good.'

'So, what now?'

'Come on, you two,' Harry called back to them from deep inside a tangle of wires. 'Get yourselves ready!'

'Ready for what?' asked Callum. 'There's nobody here!'

But just as the words left Callum's mouth, Adam spotted a few faces cautiously peeking around the corners of the surrounding buildings.

Harry spotted them too, and freed himself from his tangle of wires to re-join Adam and Callum. 'People are curious!' he whispered. 'But they won't come out until they know what's going on. Until they feel safe. This kind of thing is totally new to us, remember! Lots of people, nocubicles ... they'll be nervous! So *go*, up onstage, both of you, and make it impossible for them to walk away!'

Adam's legs no longer felt like jelly due to exhaustion, they now felt like jelly because he was so *nervous*. Bizarrely, with everything they'd had to plan and arrange over the last few days, they'd hardly had any time to actually plan what they were going to do once they were up onstage. There were only three things they had prepared:

1. Costumes – the banana suit for Callum, and a pair of stilts for Adam (he'd mastered stilts a few months back, after scaring the life out of Callum in a 'GIANT Teddy Bear Outside Little Bro's Bedroom Window' prank video).

2. Tubas. Neither of them had any idea how to play them, but that didn't matter because of the next part of their plan …

3. Yes, people would be expecting to see music, moneysaving tips, and about the new NAL revolution, but Adam knew that before they could do any of that, he and Callum would have to put people at ease, get them to relax,

earn their confidence, and Adam only knew
one way of doing that — get them having *fun*.

So, up onstage, now fully dressed in their costumes,
and tubas in their hands, they began their perform-
ance in front of Harry, Ethan, Bruce, and some very
distant onlookers.

'Good morning, everyone!' Adam's voice echoed
on and on around the empty square. 'It's so nice to
see so many ... erm ... faces, like, peering around
street corners!'

Ethan, Bruce and Harry clapped their hands furiously, which was the applause equivalent of the
New Year's Eve fireworks display being replaced
by one man lobbing a half-finished sparkler in
the air.

'What an amazing welcome! Thank you! My
name is Adam B, and this is my little brother,
Callum, and together ... we ... are ...'

'YOU TUBAS!' they both cheered as one.

Again, a tiny smattering of applause spluttered
from the three pairs of hands at the front of the
stage.

'Thank you so much! Thank you. We ... err ... love you all, too.' Adam's forced smile was beginning to wane and he was struggling to stay enthusiastic.

'You're such a great audience. And to thank you all for showing up, we'd like to treat you to a little song and dance routine we like to call ...'

'THE MACARENA!' Adam and Callum bellowed in unison.

They had been hoping that this would get a huge cheer of approval from the onlookers, but it didn't quite go as planned –

'Woooooh!' whooped Harry, with a never-ending echo that seemed to mock them with every reply.

'The Maca-*what?*' Adam heard Ethan whisper to Bruce.

'No idea,' Bruce whispered back.

'It's a ... erm ... like ... a, kind of, song and dance number. You might not have heard of it, but it's pretty popular where we come from, and I promise you, within twenty seconds, you'll be singing and dancing along and having the time of your lives! So, are you ready to do this?'

'Oh, absolutely, yes!' Harry's voice said at least twelve times as it bounced from wall to wall.

'I said ... ARE YOU READY TO DO THIS?!'

'OH, ABSOLUTELY, YES!' Harry replied again.

'THEN LET'S DO IT!'

Callum, who had taken ten whole weeks of trumpet lessons three years ago, put his lips to his tuba, and prepared to blow everyone's minds with his musical awesomeness. Adam, who had memorised every move to the Macarena at the age of eight, took centre stage, and prepared to introduce this altiverse to a dance extravaganza. What happened next was without a doubt the most unforgettable show ever performed in *any* universe! Unforgettable for all the wrong reasons ...

Callum very quickly learnt that playing the Macarena on the tuba is *nothing like* playing Three Blind Mice on the trumpet and made a noise that sounded like a small elephant having dental surgery. Then he stumbled around in his banana costume, fell over, got squashed beneath his own tuba and couldn't get up, so he decided to wriggle around on the stage like a banana-shaped beetle on its back.

Adam soon realised that dancing the Macarena in a pair of stilts while holding an extremely heavy tuba is *completely impossible*. He managed to complete a tiny pelvic thrust, then lift one leg in the air, before completely losing balance and stumbling all over the stage while making a noise in his tuba that sounded like a large elephant having difficulties on the toilet.

It was all going horribly wrong, yet at the same time, it was going unimaginably well. They may not have been getting people to have the times of their lives by joining in with the greatest song and dance routine of all time, but Adam and Callum were getting people to have fun in another way – people were laughing at them! Adam and Callum's disastrous mishaps were evoking howls of hilarity from the onlookers, who were slowly drifting closer and closer to the stage, no longer in their dozens but now in their *hundreds*.

Adam and Callum, meanwhile, had no idea how perfectly terribly they were doing because Callum

was too busy trying to get up off his back, and Adam was too busy trying to reach down to help him up. The only problem with this was, way up on his stilts, Adam couldn't quite bend low enough to reach Callum's outstretched hand, and the more he tried, the more he wobbled, and the more he wobbled, the more the crowd laughed, until Adam, looking like a giant spider trying to do the splits, somehow managed to stoop low enough to reach Callum's fingertips, and then – *whooompah!* Adam fell straight on top of the banana boy and got his face wedged in Callum's tuba.

When they finally got to their feet, Adam and Callum were pleasantly surprised to see Guildhall Square was *full* of onlookers – thousands of them! – and each and every one of them was in stitches. Adam could hardly believe his eyes! It worked! People had gathered! But Adam didn't allow himself to get complacent. He knew this was only the first and smallest hurdle of many yet to come. People may have been having fun, but they weren't having a good time *together*. Nobody was laughing with the person standing next to them, no one was talking to anyone else, nobody was even *looking* at one another. Adam knew that getting them all talking into the tin cups was going to be a HUGE challenge. He untangled himself from Callum's tuba, removed his stilts, got to his feet, then took a deep breath.

'Here goes nothing,' he said to himself, and then he did something that caused gasps of shock to ripple through the ever-growing crowd – he *looked* at them, *directly* at them, making eye contact with as many of them as possible.

'Hi,' he said to them, gently, as he looked from one person to the next. 'How you doing?' Kindness and sincerity oozed from every syllable. 'You OK there? Thank you for coming.'

And then he looked out at the huge mass of people, taking in the entire crowd, addressing them all –

'Wow!' Adam called out over a tin-cup megaphone. 'So many of you! Thank you! Thank you for coming to see us.' Silence. If Adam had closed his eyes, he could have believed that not a single other person was there.

'I guess the secret's out – we're not the Tuba-playing sensation you'd been expecting.'

Laughter. Adam's shoulders relaxed slightly as he breathed a sigh of relief – at least they were listening.

'But the other things we told you to expect – money-saving advice, the unveiling of the Nice and Lonely revolution – those things are true. We will be doing that because we want to help you, and we're also hoping that you might be able to help us at the same time. But we don't have long to do this, so, in a moment I'm going to tell you something that will sound completely unreal, and then we're going to *show* you something completely unreal, just to prove that the unreal is sometimes actually *real*.'

Adam leant over to Callum and whispered something to him. Callum shook his head, looking worried. Adam pleaded. Insisted. And then, finally, Adam gave Callum the phone, and Callum held it up in the air as Adam spoke to the crowd again.

'The thing I have to tell you is this – my little brother Callum and I are not from this universe. We are from somewhere very similar to your world, but where there are little differences, like, for example, we have completely different technology to you.'

There was a smattering of laughter, a murmur of confusion as people tried to figure out if this was supposed to be a joke or not. And then Adam continued. He turned his back to the audience to face a camera telescopia, and his image appeared thirty feet tall on the front wall of the Guildhall. Callum passed him the phone, and Adam held it up in front of the telescopia so that the screen was almost as big as the huge building.

'And the thing I have to show is *this* …'

Adam pressed 'play' on the phone, and the crowd instantly gave cries of surprise to see a video that Callum had just filmed, that very minute – a video of Adam, just seconds earlier, addressing that very same crowd – *'My little brother Callum and I are not from this universe. We are from somewhere very similar to your world, but where there are little differences, like, for example, we have completely different technology to you.'*

Adam instantly powered the phone back off as the battery dropped down to two per cent.

'Unbelievable!' shocked voices cried out from the audience.

'*Moving* pictures!'

'And *sound*!'

'Like magic!'

A grin of satisfaction spread across Adam's face, not just to see that people weren't disbelieving him, but also to see that not everyone in the audience was simply shouting comments towards the stage. Some of them were talking to *each other*!

'It's working!' Callum whispered.

'There's another difference in our universe,' Adam continued, startling the audience as his voice boomed out through the tin-cup megaphone again, 'we don't live in a NAL society.'

This caused an even greater gasp than the video!

'Where we come from, being lonely isn't really a nice thing at all,' Adam confessed. 'In fact, we actually *like* spending time with other people, talking, telling each other what's going on in our lives. We even have this saying – "A problem shared is a problem halved".'

Adam gave them a moment to chew this over, and what had been shock and outrage and confusion within the crowd slowly became intrigue and a desire to know more.

'And that's where the NAL revolution *and* our moneysaving tips come in. I believe – *we* believe – that if you all give it a go, if you lead this NAL revolution right now, if you stop trying to be lonely all of the time, if you start sharing your problems with each other, spending a little more time in each other's company, you won't need to buy *nearly* as many Tear-sues, because you won't feel like you're going through nearly as many problems. And you won't need to buy nearly as many Cuddle Gnomes either, because you will begin to feel loved by *other human beings*, not just stuffed toys. And you can all give it a go, right here, right now, and you can help get us back home, to our mum, who will be going through huge problems of her own right now, wondering where we've been all week, worrying about us, fearing the worst ... You see, that piece of technology we just showed you, *that* is the thing that will send us back home, but the thing is, it runs on information. That's why you can see all of these tin cups in front of you. They're all connected by wires to this little device, and if you can all talk into these tin cups, to *each other*, about facts and information,

313

maybe even sharing your problems, then that should create enough power to send us back home, to our own universe, to our *mum*.'

As Adam said this last word, he glanced down at alti-Mum, who was forcing her way to the front of the audience, with a huge smile on her face. Adam smiled back, but his smile suddenly vanished when a horrifying realisation occurred to him –

'Callum, alti-Mum is here!' he whispered.

'I know, I saw her!' Callum replied, beaming from ear to ear.

'No, Cal, think about it. We left her back at Stephington Industries, slowing down the Kilters for us,' Adam reminded him. 'So, if she's here, then ...'

'Stan and Steph Kilter could be here, too!' Callum gasped in horror.

'Exactly. So, remember, keep one eye on the lookout for them, and the other eye on Bruce.'

'Erm ... bad news,' said Callum, nervously chewing his lip. 'Bruce is nowhere to be seen.'

Adam whipped around to face the spot where Bruce had been standing, alongside Ethan and Harry, but Callum was right – Bruce was gone.

'Then we better do this, and *fast*, before the Kilter family get a chance to sabotage the entire thing!'

Adam brought the megaphone back to his lips once again.

'I know this feels pretty radical for you guys, talking, sharing feelings, that kind of stuff, but trust me, there's nothing to it,' Adam gently assured them. 'Here, I'll start it off …'

Adam picked up a silver cup from the front of the stage, and, remembering how Ethan and Bruce's slow and steady projection shows paid off, he spoke into the cup in a similarly robotic way.

'Erm … My name is Adam Beales. I've lived in Derry my whole life … kind of. My favourite colour is electric blue. And I love that I can reach out to people over the internet.'

Adam glanced down at the memory stick on a small table in front of him and noticed that its red light was already beginning to glow faintly.

Keep going, Adam! he told himself. *Get them talking! This is going to work!*

'I … err … my favourite food is … Sunday roast. And popcorn. Not together. My mum and dad are Harry and Ed—' Adam saw alti-Mum's ears prick up as he let Harry's name slip out of his mouth, then almost said her name, too.

She can't know! I can't mess with destiny! 'I mean ... Yes ... My mum and dad are ... *hairy-hannnnnded*. They have very hairy hands. And my brother ...'

Adam paused. After the last comment he noticed that the red light on the memory stick had stopped glowing and gone back to blinking. It had stopped working!

Because it wasn't a fact! Mum and Dad don't have hairy hands! It has to be true! It's not real information if it's not true!

'My brother ... doesn't have hairy hands. He is ... actually, he's awesome. I never tell him that, but he is. In fact, I never tell him anything good. I usually just complain at him, tell him he's doing everything wrong, and I never listen to what he has to say, but that's all going to change now, Callum. I promise. I love you, little bro. Now it's your turn to speak, because I think I've said enough. Oh, by the way ...' Adam addressed the audience. 'It's very important that what we all talk about, into these tin cups, is true. None of this will work and we'll never get back home if what we talk about isn't true. Real news only, please. Over to you, Callum.'

Adam offered the megaphone to Callum, but he was too busy wiping his eyes with the palms of his hands to be able to speak right at that moment.

'Err … looks like Callum might need to take a beat, so how about you guys take over from here? Give it a go, yeah?'

Adam stepped back and looked out at the endless crowd that had amassed from miles around, and he waited for them to speak.

'Anyone?' Adam pleaded. 'Just a few words? Please?'

Adam had never seen anything like it. So many people, yet the city was absolutely silent. He was pretty sure that he literally heard a pin drop. Not a single person was speaking. Not even to *each other*.

A panicked sweat began to prickle Adam's skin. He didn't know what else to do! How else could he get them talking? Even he didn't know what to say!

He looked down at the memory stick, and its glowing light had disappeared completely. It just blinked, short little blips, with very long gaps in between, like its pulse was slowing down.

This isn't going to work! These people are never going to talk!

'Ahem,' a voice echoed through the square.

Adam's eyes widened in hope! He, like everyone else, whipped his head from left to right, trying to see where the voice had come from.

'Excuse me. My name is Officer Burbank, and I very much have something to say.'

The crowd looked instantly terrified. People began backing away. Worried voices began muttering in panic –

'The police!'

'We shouldn't be here!'

'Against the law!'

'We have to go!'

'I'm not here to get anyone in trouble,' said the voice. 'In fact, quite the opposite.'

The speaker hopped up on to the steps of the hall, and Adam finally saw who it was – the police officer they'd spoken to after their first catastrophic journey on a cubicle bus. She was facing the crowd and talking into a tin cup.

'Something very sad happened in my life, not too long ago, and I didn't quite know how to deal with it. It felt like a dark cloud was following me everywhere I went, and I couldn't get rid of it. But then I met these two boys, Adam and Callum. Although … I'm pretty sure one of them was a *mother* rather than a *brother* on that day. Anyway, that's not important. What is important is that they gave me a very useful piece of advice. They told me that "a problem shared is a problem halved". And they suggested that, instead of bottling my problems up, maybe I might feel better if I talked about my feelings with someone. So I did. And that person I spoke to also shared their feelings with me. And it's *true*, I *did* start to feel better! And I've been finding that the more I talk to people, the happier I feel, and the happier it seems to make *them* feel too!'

Adam looked down at the memory stick and saw that it was glowing bright and strong.

'I also met one of these boys, just yesterday,' said another voice.

Callum gave a laugh and clapped his hands when he saw the old man from the bus climb up on to the steps of the Guildhall.

'I lost my dear Bessie last month, and it was more than I could bear. I had never felt so lonely in my life. And then this boy, little Callum, broke every rule that we live by – he stepped into my bus cubicle and he asked if I was OK. He *spoke to me*. The first person to properly speak to me since dear Bessie passed away. And suddenly I remembered that kindness still exists. And that thought reminded me that happiness also still exists. And, he doesn't know it, but that was the first time I had smiled in over six weeks.'

The light on the memory stick was brighter than ever, and Callum was wiping his eyes once again.

'Pssssst! Adam! The phone!'

Adam turned to see Ethan at the side of the stage, desperately trying to get his attention.

'Your dad says to plug the phone into the memory stick and turn it on!'

'I totally forgot! Thanks, Ethan!'

Adam powered Callum's phone up, and plugged it into Harry's homemade cable that trailed from the other end of the memory stick. The second it turned on, the battery level dropped from two per cent to one per cent.

Oh no.

'It's true!' a third voice piped up. This time it was alti-Mum. 'My name is Edelle Crawley. My favourite colour is ... I don't actually have just one favourite colour. I like so many. And, if I'm being completely honest, I've *never* liked living in our NAL society. Nice and Lonely? Really? What's so nice about being lonely? It's true what these boys are saying – a problem shared really *is* a problem halved! Since I met these boys, I've begun talking to someone in a way that I've never spoken to anyone in my life! And I LOVE IT!'

Adam noticed that Edelle was looking directly at Harry, and that Harry's blushing face was glowing almost as brightly as the light on the memory stick.

'I prefer being at work to being at home!' someone in the crowd called out. 'Because I like being around people!'

'I eat my lunch in the park and imagine that all the other people there are my friends!' another person yelled.

'I want to cuddle *people* as well as stuffed gnomes!'

'I prefer laughing to crying!'

'My favourite food is pizza, but I like it better when it's shared!'

'Our house is too empty!' Ethan's mum cried out. 'It's BORING! I want to be able to have friends round!'

And, just like that, *everyone* was talking. And they weren't just talking, they were *smiling*. Laughing, even! Saying things they'd been wanting to say their entire lives!

Adam looked out at the joy they had inspired, and he felt happier than ever before.

'Adam!' Callum called out. 'Look at the phone!'

Adam's stomach lurched as he forced himself to peer at the phone's screen, half expecting it to have completely run out of battery and shut down, but then his heart flipped when something else popped up on the screen –

'Callum! We have a Wi-Fi bar!'

'*What*?!' Callum gasped. 'How is that even possible?'

'It's working, Cal! All of this information – the phone thinks it's connected to the internet!'

'And if the *phone* thinks it's connected to the internet, that means the memory stick does too!'

'YES!' Adam cheered.

The noise of the crowd was now *deafening*! You couldn't stop them talking if you'd tried! Every single person was opening their hearts into their silver cups, and the atmosphere literally felt electric.

'CALLUM! LOOK! THE PHONE!'

Both brothers put their arms around each other as the Wi-Fi signal grew to two bars, then *three*, and then it started to happen – the screen began to glow white, and a high-pitched electrical beep began to ring out.

'POPULARIS IS BACK!' Callum whooped. 'We just need to tell it what we want!'

And then …

The glowing screen began to dim.

The beeping stopped. The whistling died away.

The Wi-Fi bars started to drop.

'NO!' Adam gasped. 'Something's wrong!'

'I don't get it!' Callum wailed. 'The people are still talking! The wires are still connected! I can't see what's wrong.'

But Adam had a horrible feeling he knew *exactly* what was wrong.

'Where is Bruce?' he yelled over the verbal thunder of thousands of people all speaking into their tin cups at once.

They looked all around. They could see Harry, they could see Ethan, both busy divulging their own stories into the tin cups, but Bruce was nowhere to be found.

'He's up to something!' Adam shouted. 'I know he is! We have to find him!'

The brothers searched everywhere, out in the crowd, under the stage, over by the control box for the lights, but Bruce had vanished.

'Wait!' cried Callum. 'Over there! I see him!'

Callum was pointing to the left side of the stage, where Bruce was scarpering like a mouse from a cat.

'*What* is he doing?' bellowed Adam.

'He's heading backstage, Adam! We have to stop him!' Callum wailed. 'The battery's going to die any second now!'

Adam began racing towards the back of the stage, to head Bruce off before he got there, and then he spotted what it was that Bruce was heading for, and his heart ran cold at what he saw –

Stan and Steph Kilter were both huddled around a silver cup, spouting out as many lies as they could, as fast as possible.

'The sky is yellow!'

'The grass is pink!'

'One plus one is eight!'

'Nobody here is happy!'

'Loneliness is best!'

'Keep your feelings locked inside and your troubles learn to run and hide!'

'They're lying!' Callum yelled. 'They're stopping it from working with fake facts! We have to stop them!'

'We have to stop Bruce before he helps them!' Adam added. He ran as fast as he could, but Bruce was faster, charging around the back of the stage like a supercharged bull.

The glow of the phone's screen was almost gone!

The high-pitched beep nearly dead!

The Wi-Fi bars were down to one!

Adam was finally drawing level with Bruce! He dug his heels in, ready to launch himself off the stage at him, when …

A hand grabbed the back of Adam's hood, dragging him to a halt.

'NOOOOOOO!' Adam roared.

He turned to yell at whoever had stopped him, but when he saw who it was, all hope left his body, to be replaced by a sickening feeling of betrayal, deep down in his soul, accompanied a painful pang of heartbreak.

'Harry? Ethan?' he whimpered. '*Why?*'

Harry simply carried on smiling, then pointed down to Bruce, who was careening towards his parents, at top speed.

'You don't need to stop him,' Harry assured him.

'He's a good guy, remember?' added Ethan. 'Look!'

Held tight in the clutches of his best friend and alti-dad, Adam watched helplessly as the Bruce-shaped blur thundered away from him; as the Bruce-shaped blur gave an almighty battle cry; as the Bruce-shaped blur *ploughed into his own parents*, knocking Stan and Steph Kilter away like skittles before picking up a silver cup for himself.

'MY NAME IS BRUCE KILTER! I'M THIRTEEN YEARS OLD! MY FAVOURITE COLOUR IS PINK! AND I AM TIRED OF HAVING PARENTS WHO CARE MORE ABOUT MAKING MONEY THAN MAKING FRIENDS! THINGS ARE GOING TO CHANGE AROUND HERE! I'M GOING TO BE MAKING SOME RULES, MYSELF! STARTING RIGHT NOW!'

Bruce raised a fist into the air, saluting Adam and Callum, whose cheers of delight were drowned out by the deafening roar of the crowd, who, watching on, celebrated like they'd just won the World Cup.

'BRUCE!' Adam called down to him. 'YOU'RE A TOTAL LEGEND! I'M SORRY FOR EVER DOUBTING YOU!'

'BRUUUUUUUUCE!' Ethan cheered as he leaped from the stage, straight onto Bruce's back, and wrapped his arms around his friend, like he was the world's biggest Cuddle Gnome. 'You absolute BEAUTY!'

'GO!' Bruce ordered Adam and Callum as he ruffled Ethan's hair. 'It's happening! GOOD LUCK!'

And he wasn't wrong.

The phone screen was glowing white once more, and the high-pitched beep was growing to a deafening screech.

'Look!' Callum howled with laughter as he pointed to the screen of his phone, where the only things visible apart from a dazzling white light were the Wi-Fi bars. 'Three bars! A full signal!'

The crowd were cheering their facts into the tin cups, jumping and dancing as they did so, and then the impossible happened.

'FOUR BARS!' Callum cheered.

'*What?*' laughed Adam. 'You can't even *get* four bars! It only goes to three!'

'*FIVE* bars!' Callum whooped.

Adam looked at the phone and couldn't believe what he was seeing – the phone really did have *five* bars of Wi-Fi!

'Looks like it's working!' came a voice from the front of the stage.

Adam looked up to see Harry and Edelle – alti-Mum and alti-Dad – smiling up at him and Callum.

'We can't thank you guys enough!' Adam called down to them.

'No,' Harry called back. 'We're the ones who should be thanking *you*! Things are going to be much better around here, thanks to you two!'

'He's probably right!' Edelle agreed with a huge laugh. 'But I have absolutely NO IDEA what is going on right …' Edelle stopped mid-sentence when she caught sight of Callum's phone and her eyes widened in recognition. '*That's* why you two look so familiar! You're the aliens who came into my house!'

Adam gave a grimace of apology. 'Erm … about that …'

'Never mind!' Edelle yelled with a smile. 'You can explain next time you visit!'

'But wait! Dad! There's something we need to tell you,' Callum yelled down to them.

'No, Callum, you need to go!' Harry told him with a warm smile. 'We're going to be just fine!'

Harry put an arm around Edelle, and Edelle wrapped both her arms around Harry.

'We'll be *better* than fine!' Edelle assured them. 'And so will you, as long as you remember that a problem shared is a problem halved.'

Harry pulled out a pack of Tear-sues from his pocket and tossed them into a bin.

'I'm definitely not going to be needing quite so many of those any more!'

The phone was blindingly bright. The beeping was tearing at Adam's ears. The battery wouldn't be able to take much more! The jubilant crowd watched on in amazement.

'YOU NEED TO MAKE YOUR WISH!' Harry bellowed.

Adam nodded. He held on to Callum's hand, turned to Ethan, gave him a goodbye wink, then looked into his dad's eyes as he said the words –

'Popularis ... take us home!'

Nothing happened. Not yet.

All eyes were on Callum.

'You need to say it too, Cal!' Adam reminded him.

'But ... *Dad* ...'

Callum's lip wobbled.

Harry smiled up at him, his eyes glistening with tears.

'You can do this, son.'

'But ...'

'I know I'm not there in your universe. I saw it in your eyes. I saw it in how you only have old photos of me on your phone. But, Cal, trust me, go back home and *talk* to your mum about me. A problem shared is a problem halved.'

Callum nodded, causing his tears to drip from his chin. Then, without taking his eyes from his dad, he managed to splutter four simple words ...

'Popularis ... take me home.'

A supernova of light exploded from the phone.

Adam saw the screen break into a million pieces.

And then he saw the same thing happen to Callum's heart.

17

No Place Like Home

With a stomach-spinning lurch, Adam hurtled through dimension after dimension before landing safe and sound back in his own familiar universe, which was drenched in sunrise. Safe and sound back in his own version of Derry, where he felt his heart slotting back into place like a missing piece of a jigsaw puzzle, telling him that he was home.

Safe and sound back in good old *Harrington* Industries, which was now just a pile of rubble with a few bent and twisted steel girders swaying and creaking ominously overhead, threatening to crush them both at any given moment.

'AAAAAAARRRRGGGGGHHHHHHHHH!

CALLUM! WE HAVE TO GET OUT OF HERE!'

But as he turned to grab his little brother and run, Adam realised that Callum wasn't there!

'CALLUM!' he yelled at the top of his voice.

He looked everywhere, scanning the mounds of rubble that surrounded him, but saw no sign of Callum. A burning hot panic overcame him. Where was he? Was Callum still back in the altiverse? Had Popularis accidentally sent him to the *wrong* universe? Or was he lost, floating around in nothingness, destined to be trapped between plains, all alone, for the rest of eternity? Or—

'I'm down here.'

Or was he on his knees, huddled into a ball, right next to Adam's feet?

'Callum! What are you doing down there? I thought I'd lost you! Are you OK? What's wrong?'

'Gone!' Callum spluttered between coughs and sobs. 'Forever!'

Adam crouched down and put a hand on his brother's back.

'I know Dad's gone, Cal, but I don't think *anything* is "forever". Not when we've got Popularis

standing by. I mean, I'm sure we'll be able to get in touch again somehow.'

'That's what I'm *talking* about, Adam!' Callum groaned, pushing himself up on to his knees. 'We *don't* have Popularis standing by! We left the memory stick back in the altiverse! We can't call on him ever again!'

Adam looked at both his hands, as if expecting to find the memory stick gripped in one of them. Then he checked all his pockets. But Callum was right. The memory stick was gone for good.

'Well, maybe we could make another one!'

Adam reasoned hopefully. 'The source code that was on the memory stick must have come from Dad's computer, so all we need to do is find that computer, find the source code, and put it on a new memory stick!'

'Adam,' Callum croaked sadly, looking up at his big brother as if he was two fingers short of a KitKat, 'we already found Dad's computer. It's underneath the gigantic beam you're standing on, smashed into a thousand pieces.'

'Oh. Right. Yeah. Well, in that case, I guess we could always ... RUUUUUUUUN!'

The steel girders that had been creaking and swaying above them were no longer creaking and swaying, they were now screeching and toppling. Screeching and toppling straight towards Adam and Callum! The brothers scrambled over the rubble, stumbling, falling, slipping, tripping, until finally they were standing on Harrington Lane, next to a pile of never-used lamp posts, and ...

KERRRROOOOOOOMPPPHHHHH!

Like three enormous metal trees, Adam and Callum watched as the girders crashed down into the remains of Harrington Industries, sending a cloud of dust billowing into the air.

Coughing and spluttering, the brothers ran from the wreckage and back towards their house.

'We've been gone nearly a whole week,' wheezed Callum. 'You'd think the place would have finished falling down by now!'

'Not necessarily,' said Adam, pausing to wipe the dirt from his eyes. 'A few years ago, there was an old building next to the river that took *months* to fall down. They had to send in diggers to finish it off in the end. And what about castles? Some of them have been falling down for hundreds of years and still aren't done!'

Callum stared at Adam, his eyes wide with horror.

'*Months? Years?* Adam, do you remember that film we watched, where they go to space, and when they come back home it's, like, *centuries* later? You don't think that could have happened to *us* do you? You don't think there's been some kind of weird quantum time shift and we've actually been gone months or years?'

Adam wanted to say, 'Nah, don't be stupid, that would *never* happen!' But he knew the terrified look on his face told Callum otherwise.

'P-probably not,' he stammered instead. 'But let's go home, just to check. You know, like, *right now*.'

So Adam and Callum raced back home – across deserted car parks, past abandoned buildings, through the overgrown scrap metal yard – until they were finally back outside their good old dirty, greyish, brownish white front door. Callum was about to burst inside, but Adam put a hand out to stop him.

'Wait,' Adam whispered. 'What if time *has* moved strangely while we've been away? It happens in all the books, all the films – what felt like a few days to us could have been a few *years* back here! We can't just go bursting into the house screaming, "We're home!" What if Mum thinks we've been dead all this time? What if Mum's an *old lady* now? We could give her a heart attack! We have to go in carefully, *quietly*.'

'Ughhhh, whatever,' groaned Callum in reluctant agreement as he pushed open the door and crept inside.

As they stepped onto the raggedy hall carpet, Adam drew a breath of relief to see the usual mess of shoes behind the door, the walls still littered with family photos, and a dozen of Callum's hoodies strewn over the bannisters and up the stairs.

'However long we've been gone, it's definitely not been years,' Adam whispered. 'Probably not even *weeks*.'

They crept from room to room and were pleased to see that nothing much seemed to have changed since they had left. Nothing, that is, except for one tiny detail – there was absolutely no sign of Mum.

'Maybe she's in the garden,' suggested Callum.

But the garden was empty and eerily silent.

'Upstairs bathroom?' said Adam.

But that was empty, too, and even weirder – the loft hatch was still open from when Callum had gone up and found the memory stick, on the morning they disappeared.

'I don't like this, Adam,' Callum muttered, panic rising in his voice.

'Me neither,' said Adam. 'Something's not right. We've been gone all this time, and Mum's not touched a single thing!'

'You don't think … something's happened to her, do you?' Callum whispered meekly.

All of the different possibilities raced through Adam's mind:

Is she out searching for us?

Gone to stay at Aunt Jenna's while the police try to solve our disappearance?

Do they think our house is a CRIME SCENE? Have the police KEPT her out?

Or is she a suspect in our disappearance? Has Mum been arrested?!

And then the worst thought of all dawned on him: *What if we weren't the only ones who got zapped to an alternate universe?!*

Panic surged through Adam's veins. He didn't know what to do! He raced back to the stairs. Paused to think. Turned and dashed to the bathroom again.

'She's not here, Adam,' Callum whimpered. 'What do we do?'

Adam clutched at his hair.

'I don't know, Cal!' he admitted tearfully. 'I don't know!'

And then it occurred to him – 'Of course!' He'd spent so long without a phone he had almost forgotten how they worked! 'I'll call her!'

With his own phone out of battery all week, and Callum's still back in the altiverse along with the memory stick, he dashed towards the stairs to use the landline phone in the kitchen, but he didn't even get halfway across the landing before something caused him to freeze on the spot – *a noise*!

'What was *that*?' Callum whispered fearfully.

Adam didn't answer. He listened, trying to ignore the hammering of his own heart.

What was *it?*

A snarl?

A growl?

A ...

Adam and Callum both leaped a foot in the air when the sound came again. Much louder, this time, and there was no mistaking where it was coming from. The room directly behind them – *Mum's room.* Slowly, tentatively, Adam turned around to find himself looking directly at the creature responsible for the noise, and then a smile spread across his face.

'It's *Mum!*' he quietly gasped.

'What's *wrong* with her?' Callum demanded, not daring to look. 'Why's she making those noises?!'

'She's asleep, Cal!' Adam laughed. 'She's *snoring.*'

Barely believing what they were seeing (and barely believing their own stupidity at not even looking for their mum in her *own bedroom*), Adam and Callum tiptoed inside. There she was – Mum – fast asleep. Not an old lady. Not even *nearly* an old lady. She looked almost exactly the same as when they'd last seen her.

Adam's heart ached to see that, even while she was sleeping, she had a crease of worry on her brow. Instinctively, Adam gently smoothed the crease away, stroking his mum's forehead the same way she used to stroke his when he was ill or upset. Callum perched on the edge of the bed and held her hand in his, and like Sleeping Beauty woken by two Prince Charmings, their mum slowly opened her eyes. She looked at Adam, then to Callum, and her eyes widened.

'Am I still dreaming?' she whispered.

Callum smiled down at her, his eyes glistening with tears as, gently he told her – 'No, Mum, it's *real*. We're here, and it's *really* real!'

Their mum half sat up as she gazed all around her, to the window, the door, the clock, then back to her sons, as if trying to take it all in. Her eyes widened even more. Fully awake now, her mouth dropped open.

'It's really real?' she whispered in disbelief.

'Yes!' Adam confirmed with a nod.

Mum looked shell-shocked.

'You mean … You mean … it's my day off work, and I've been woken up at six a.m. BY A FOUR-FOOT TALKING BANANA?! Are you two *kidding me*?! If this is another one of your prank videos I will be SO ANGRY!'

'*What?!*' Callum squealed in protest. 'We've been gone for almost a whole week, and *that's* all you've got to say? Didn't you miss us *at all*?'

'*Miss* you? A *week*? What are you blathering on about?! I saw you just before I went to bed! *Last night!* Which wasn't long enough ago, so please get out of my room, so I can get some sleep!'

'Last night?' Adam gasped. 'Are you serious?'

'Yes, Adam, I am *deadly* serious! Now, scram, the pair of you, and don't wake me up for at least another three hours. And if you're secretly filming me right now and I see this on YouTube tomorrow, you will both be in *serious* trouble. Got it?'

'So there *was* a quantum time shift!' Adam laughed, clapping and arm around Callum's banana-curved back. 'But instead of it making time go slower *here*, it made time go slower in the *altiverse*, meaning we managed to squeeze a whole *week* of altiverse time into just a few *minutes* of *our* time!'

'Yeah, sure,' said Callum, condescendingly patting his big brother on the back. 'Either that or when we told Popularis to send us 'back' it actually sent us *back* back, like, back to the exact time and place that we disappeared from. Just a thought.'

'Will you two please discuss your sci-fi nonsense somewhere that *isn't* the room that I'm trying to be asleep in?'

Their mum complained and protested, but it was no use. Adam and Callum had simply missed her too much to be able to leave her alone right now, so they cosied up to her on the bed, wrapped their arms around her, and told her the whole sci-fi-nonsense story. Well, the first *sixty seconds* of their sci-fi-nonsense story, at least, until Mum interrupted them. 'Wonderful. Great. I've never heard such a load of rubbish in my life. I don't believe a word of it. Now are you going to let me sleep, or not?'

'Not,' Callum admitted.

'Sorry, Mum,' said Adam with a helpless shrug.

This was not what she what she wanted to hear, but she soon softened up when Callum turned to her and said, 'Mum? Please can you tell me about Dad?'

She sighed and she moaned, pretending to be annoyed, but Adam could see in her eyes that there was nothing she would like to do more.

'Well, what do you want to know?' she asked.

'*Everything*,' Callum whispered. 'You see, I've had this problem for a while – I'm starting to feel like I'm forgetting him, or maybe I could never really remember him properly in the first place, and I *want* to remember him. I want to feel like I know him better than I ever did.'

Mum gave Callum a very serious stare.

'Then you're talking to the right person, because your dad is in here,' she pointed to her head, 'and he's in here,' she pointed to her heart, 'and he's also in *here*.' She gave Callum an almighty hug. And then she began.

She told Callum and Adam all about how she had first met their dad, what he was like, what they talked about, and apart from the occasional toilet break, or a quick dash to the kitchen for some tea and toast, the three of them stayed like that for hours, until Mum reached the very end of the story – the last time she saw him, in the hospital. And by the time she was done, Adam could see that Callum's new knowledge made him feel as though his dad was now in his *own* head, his own heart.

'Thanks, Mum,' Callum whispered as he smiled contentedly up at the ceiling.

'Feel better now?' she asked.

'Much. And you know what else I was thinking ... WAIT!' Callum sat bolt upright, as if he'd just found the solution to world hunger. 'Go back! The thing you just told us about when you got married – the *vows*. What did you say Dad said?'

Mum gave a bemused smile as she recounted Dad's marriage vows. 'He said, "I, Harrington Paul Beales, hereby declare—"'

'Dad's actual name was *Harrington*?' Adam gasped, realising the same thing as Callum.

'Harry – short for Harrington,' Mum confirmed. 'Did you two honestly not know that?'

But Adam and Callum were already out of the room, racing to the printer beneath Callum's desk, out of which Adam snatched up one of the printouts that had begun the whole adventure.

'Callum! Popularis's riddle! *Look!*'

Callum leant in close, and the two of them pored over the page.

To succeed in your mission, you must go to the top
Explore what's on offer, and don't ever stop
The answer's in Harrington, what you wish you must speak
Only then shall you win the prize that you seek

'We both thought that "Harrington" was just the name of the street.' Adam squealed with excitement. 'But it wasn't.'

'It was talking about *Dad*!' blurted Callum. '"*What you wish you must speak*" didn't mean to go to Harrington Lane and say my wish out loud, it meant to *speak Dad's name*!'

'To talk about Dad!' Adam confirmed. 'And "*To succeed in your mission, you must go to the top*" didn't mean go up to the *loft*, it meant go to the top of the *family*. It was talking about *Mum*!'

'It was telling me to go to Mum, and talk about Dad.'

'"*Only then shall you win the prize that you seek*",' Adam concluded.

'Adam,' Callum whispered in disbelief, 'the answer was right here in this riddle all along. I just translated it wrong!'

'And all the rest – the memory stick, the altiverse, the "NAL revolution" stuff – it was all just an *accident*!'

'A freak coincidence!' Callum laughed.

'Well, we got there in the end, I suppose,' Adam chuckled, slapping a hand on his brother's shoulder. 'We just took a really long time figuring it out.'

'Why did Popularis have to use a riddle?' Callum complained. 'Why didn't it just spell it out in plain English. *The best way to get to know Dad better is to talk to Mum about him.* It would have been so much easier!'

'A whole lot less fun too, though,' Adam pointed out.

Callum chuckled with embarrassment and slapped his hand into his forehead. 'We spent a whole week in an alternate universe, worried we might never get home again, just so we could learn the one thing Mum's been telling us for years …'

And then, in perfect unison, the two of them said it together …

'A problem shared is a problem halved!'

A ridiculous amount of relieved laughter followed.

'Callum, do you reckon alti-Dad's OK? Did we actually make a difference there, or do you think everyone in the altiverse has gone back to being sad and lonely again?' Adam asked.

It was very late that evening, and Adam and Callum were preparing to hunker down to bed for the night … in the shed at the bottom of their garden. Mum had looked at them a bit weirdly when they'd told her the plan ('First *my* room all day, then the shed this evening? What's wrong with your *actual* bedrooms?!'), but they'd waved her off and told her that they were doing it for a video and she'd accepted it readily enough.

'I wish we had some way of knowing,' Adam went on, resting his head awkwardly on a bag of compost. Their shed wasn't quite as roomy as alti-Ethan's. 'Popularis would have been able to tell us. If only we'd been able to bring the source code memory stick back with us, or the beam hadn't destroyed the computer back at Harrington Industries …'

From Callum's wistful expression, Adam could tell that he was having similar thoughts. But he was clearly determined to put a brave face on the situation. 'Well,' he said cheerily, 'we might never know what's going on in the altiverse – but I'm up to date on what's going on in *this* universe, and I think you're going to like it. Look at THIS!' Callum passed Adam his phone, which was fully charged and operational once more. 'I just checked our channel, and we're at ten million subscribers!'

Callum was right – their epic London skyscraper video was a certified banger and had tipped them over the edge! It had raked in a whopping three and a half million views in just over twenty-four hours. Adam still couldn't get his head around that – it felt like they'd filmed that video a lifetime ago. In a way, he supposed, they had.

'So what's next for the B-Boys?' Callum was saying. 'I still want that Diamond Play Button, you know! I was thinking maybe we should go back to our roots, do some classic pranks. Maybe I'll surprise you with some that you'll never see coming!' He leant past several spades and forty-seven flower pots to give Adam a playful shove. 'Perhaps I'll draw on your face with marker pen, or fill your socks with jelly, or – OUCH! What's that in my suit?'

Adam watched in confusion as Callum drew out a strangely familiar boxy-looking object from the tip of his banana suit, which he'd refused to take off even for sleep.

'What the heck?!' Callum said, gazing at it. 'That definitely wasn't there earlier, it would have fallen out when I went for a wee. How did – HEY!' he yelled.

Adam had jumped up, sending packets of seeds cascading everywhere, and snatched the object from Callum's grasp.

'Callum! Don't you see what this is! It's one of Harry's camera telescopia! And it's glowing!'

'But ... that's impossible – you're not even focusing it at anything!'

'Hang on.' Excitedly, Adam focused the telescope part of the device at the shed's mostly empty back wall.

What he saw there took his breath away. Across the entire whitewashed wall, with crystal clarity, better and brighter than any projector, was an image of Harry's empty apartment back in the altiverse.

Callum shoved at him, trying to get a better view. 'Adam! Look! There's someone coming in – it's Harry!'

'And alti-Mum!' Adam laughed as on the screen they saw Edelle emerging from Harry's innovative bin lift, looking confused and yet charmed, before heading over to Harry with a fond look in her eyes.

'Our plan worked!' Adam cried.

But that wasn't the most surprising thing. Next to emerge from the bin transportation was ...

'Bruce?!'

Callum was right. They watched as their actually-not-a-nemesis-after-all put down the giant backpack he was carrying and gazed at the huge apartment, with all its gadgets and wild inventions, in wonder. Next, Harry came over and patted him on the shoulder, and Bruce looked back at him, smiling widely. It looked a lot like a father welcoming home his son.

'Callum!' Adam squealed. 'Do you know what this means?! Popularis must have put this in your banana suit! And if he can do *that*, it means that maybe he's still around! Maybe we can contact him, even with the source computer destroyed and the memory stick stuck in the altiverse! Maybe—'

'Adam,' Callum interrupted him, and Adam was surprised to see his little brother's eyes shining with tears. 'I'm so glad I got to see this. It must be Popularis's way of telling us Harry's going to be OK without us. He's got a whole new life to live. But let's put the camera telescopia away now. I think I'm *ready* to say goodbye to Popularis for good. I think you were right, and—'

At the sound of rustling from outside the shed, Callum shushed himself, and Adam hurriedly chucked the telescopia into a watering can with a clatter. 'Mum, is that you?' he called worriedly.

'Er, yes, only me,' Mum said, squeaking open the door and popping her head in. 'Sorry to interrupt your, erm, shed camping, but I've been thinking about what you said earlier. You know you asked me to have a think about what would make my birthday next week the best on record? Well, I know EXACTLY what I'd like to do! All this talk of sharing problems has given me the perfect idea ...'

18

Party Time!

It was a regular Saturday afternoon, just like any other. Not too hot, not too cold, just ... you know, *normal*. And Adam was just a regular thirteen-year-old boy. Not blessed with superpowers, and not totally evil or intent on taking over the world either, just ... you know, *normal*. And, currently, Adam was at the top of a giant slide outside the front of his house, wearing a huge orange jumpsuit, about to launch himself into a massive inflatable pool of custard. For Adam – Internet Sensation Extraordinaire – this was a fairly normal day ... except for the fact that he wasn't filming any of it.

When Mum had told Adam and Callum that she didn't need anything for her birthday, and that what she would really love is the opportunity to make other people happy, they had jumped at the chance.

The brothers had sprung into action. They'd rallied Ethan, gathered materials, and with the help of the community, the Mother Beales Derry Custard Slide Extravaganza began to take shape. Local businesses had chipped in (with the notable exception of Stan and Steph Kilter) to provide supplies and volunteers, and now the whole neighbourhood was buzzing with excitement for Adam and Callum to start a whole day full of activities.

The street was alive with food stalls, street games, bunting and decorations, and strung between every lamp post were dozens of different banners, each with the helpline number for local crisis charities, to raise awareness of the importance of sharing their problems.

And in the centre of all of this was Adam and Callum, atop the toweringly tall inflatable slide.

'Ladies and gentlemen, welcome to the Derry Custard Slide Extravaganza! Are you ready for the ride of your lives?' Adam yelled through a megaphone (a *regular* megaphone), his voice echoing down the street.

The crowd erupted in cheers and applause, their energy contagious. With a playful wink from next to him, Callum added, 'But remember, folks, this isn't just about fun and food and ... stuff. Every slide down the custard slide today will help raise money for local charities!'

The line of eager participants stretched the entire length of the street, people of all ages waiting for their turn into the pool of custard-y slime. Adam could have sworn he saw Bruce in there somewhere, and he didn't even seem to have any peanuts with him.

Suddenly, just as Callum and Adam were about to launch themselves face first into the gungiest bath of their lives, they heard their mum's voice rise above the crowd.

'Wait! Cal, Ad, not without me! I'm coming too,' she called as she clambered nervously up to the top of the wobbling slide. Sitting herself between her two sons, Mrs Beales held her phone out for a selfie, and Adam and Callum squeezed in.

'Cheeeeeeeese!' They both grinned.

'No, you daft pair! It's not a photo. It's a video! For my new YouTube channel – "Mama-B Charities"!'

Adam and Callum whipped their heads round to gawp at their mum in disbelief.

'A *YouTube* channel?' gasped Adam.

'*You?*' laughed Callum.

'You're not the only ones capable of doing this, thank you very much! I'm going to make a new video, once a month. Every video will be a brand-new stunt big enough to rival even *yours*, and just like today, each stunt will raise money for a different charity.'

'Wow! You kept *that* quiet!' added Adam, barely believing his ears.

'Well, I wanted to catch the looks of surprise on your faces when I told you. Mission accomplished! Now come on, are we going down this slide or are we going to …'

Mum gave a groan of annoyance as she fiddled with her phone.

'Not *again*! Stupid thing.'

'Ran out of space again?' asked Adam.

'No, it's this annoying pop-up ad that just keeps coming back, telling me to "Click the link and

Popularis will solve all of your problems". Like anyone would be stupid enough to fall for a scam like that ... *Oops*! I think I accidentally pressed "OK"! Ah, never mind, we'll fix that later. Right now we've got a video to film.'

Mum raised the camera in the air.

Adam stared at Callum.

Callum stared at Adam.

Looking into the camera, Mum called out – 'Watch out Derry, here comes Mama-B and her adorable little B-Boys! THREE ... TWO ... ONE ...'

As they pushed themselves off, Mum's phone let out an ear-splitting *BEEEEEP*, the screen flashed with a blinding white light, and Adam and Callum both cried out –

'HERE

WE

GOOOOOOOOOOO!!!'

Acknowledgements

This tale of *Adam Destroys the Internet* is a journey my brother and I share. Cyaaaallum, or as other people like to call him, Callum ... You can be a bit annoying sometimes, but most of the time (99.9% of it), you're incredibly funny, kind-hearted, and someone who I am proud to call a brother. Spending time together and going on these crazy and wacky adventures, both in real life and within these pages, means more than words can say. Watching you grow and being able to share so many life experiences with you is something I would never change for the world. Keep being you, little bro! Love you.

Of course, I have to say thanks to Mum and Dad for meeting up in real life and bringing me into the normal universe so that I can actually write this book about normal universes and alternate universes, and how you can access these fictional alternate universes through the fictional normal universes! That's a lot of universes!

Hey, Dom! Remember all those times I disappeared into my writing cave? Well, now you can see the magic that kept me hooked. Thanks for putting up with my antics. Love you for rolling with it all!

Oran O'Carroll, the visionary behind my growth; James Wills and Tom Clempson, guiding lights of unwavering support; James and David for their epic artwork; Hannah, Emily, Alesha, Fliss, Danielle, Anna, Jess, Mike and the entire Bloomsbury team (there's a long list of them), a passionate crew that turned belief into reality – your combined influence shaped this journey. Thanks to all of you for believing in my stories.

To my incredible family, friends and amazing support network – your inspirations pulse through my books. The love and encouragement you've given me are treasures I hold close and deeply appreciate. Your guidance in every step of this journey has made all the difference. Thank you.

How to draw Adam and Callum in ten short(ish) steps!

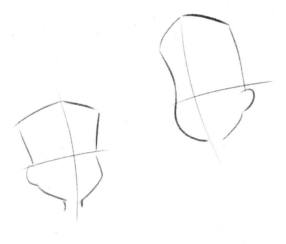

1.

Draw Adam and Callum's heads. Callum has a big old bean head and a pointed chin (sorry, Callum, Adam told me to write that). Adam's head is a long oval shape – it looks bit like he's wearing a tall hat.

2.

Add in their big round eyes, button noses,
ears that stick out and eyebrows (make Adam's
look a bit like he's been surprised that Bruce
has said something).

3.

Give the B-boys some eyeballs — they look
scary without them! — and two big cheesy smiles,
with teeth and a tongue for Adam.

4.

Draw the outline of their hair — like boxes on
top of their heads, but these will be magically
turned into curls, so make the line light.

5.

Turn those boxes into their classic curls.
Don't forget Callum's quiff (a stylish choice,
according to Mum), then shade them in.

6.

Add the bodies, but no arms ...

think Egyptian mummy vibes.

7.

Now for the arms. But we're not going to make it easy. Imagine this … Callum and Adam have just fallen from a helicopter and *survived* (with the help of a parachute, but please don't try that at home!), and now they're high-fiving to celebrate.

8.

The B-boys are in cool jeans, shoes, and hoodies that might look a bit like a neck pillow for now — try and do the outline of those outfits. Then tidy up their fingers.

9.

Finish off by giving Adam his backpack, some freckles for both of them and adding some extra details to the outfits.

10.

Shade or colour them in and ...

Voila! You should have something that looks

a bit like this:

Have you read

The first magical, record-smashing and
heartwarming tale of wish fulfilment gone
wrong from Adam B

AVAILABLE NOW

Turn the page for a sneak peek …

1

The Heroes

It was morning. Not just any morning – Adam's favourite kind:

- Sunny (for October)
- Warm (except his feet, which at age thirteen no longer fitted in the bed he'd had since he was eight)
- Lazy. Slow enough for him to gather his thoughts, try to remember his dreams, plan which YouTubers to catch up on first …
- And best of all, it was the weekend. Nothing beats a long, relaxing lie-in on a Sunday mor—

'ADAM! You better be out of bed! We're leaving in ten minutes!'

Let's start again.

It was morning. Not just any morning. Adam's least favourite kind – the kind when you think it's the weekend, when actually it's a

MONDAY!

Adam had never literally leaped out of bed before, but there's a first time for everything. He had never tried to get both his gangly legs into his school jumper, or tried to brush his teeth with the handle of his toothbrush before, but hey, give him a break, he had been a teenager for a whole six weeks now, and teenagers are supposed to be rubbish at getting up in the morning, right?

'Oh, so you *are* alive?' his frazzled-looking mum managed to joke as Adam launched himself down the stairs and did a sock-slide into the kitchen, where his mum and brother were hurriedly finishing up breakfast.

His mum grabbed her keys from the side and began making for the front door, but she didn't get far before Adam had hold of her and was spinning her around

the kitchen, doing one of his 'dances', while singing one of his 'songs'. The dance in question was an Adam classic, and mostly involved him jumping around in circles. The song was also an Adam original, and, like all his other songs, consisted of two words, bellowed in what can only be described as a 'non-tune'.

'Ohhhh ... Weeeee're ... late, we're late. We're late, we're late, we're laaaate!'

It was common for Adam to try to irritate his mum when she was already on the verge of erupting into a full-on, code red, fury extravaganza. You'd think that it would be the final straw for her, but in fact, weirdly enough, it almost never failed to make her laugh. Making people happy, even when 'happy' seemed like a million miles away, was one of Adam's greatest skills. He was a world-class cheerer-upper. Or, as his mum put it –

'You're a whirlwind of annoyingness, that's what you are!' she yelled between howls of laughter. 'Now pack it in before you make us so late that you get detention and I get fired.'

'Nice hair, Adam,' mocked Adam's brother between huge mouthfuls of toast. Callum was only two years younger than Adam, but he looked *four* years younger, acted *eight* years younger, and was a genuine contender for Adam's title of 'Whirlwind of Annoyingness No. 1'. And Adam couldn't have been prouder of that.

'How long did it take you to make it look like you just got out of bed?' chuckled Callum as he stretched his arm up in an attempt to reach all the way to the top of Adam's stratospheric head, to mess up his shock of bed-hair even more.

'Probably about as long as it took you to make

your face look like it just got pushed out of a pig's bum,' quipped Adam.

'Adam!' his mum gasped. 'Too far!'

But Callum didn't think it was too far at all – he was chuckling toast out from between his teeth, and high-fiving his big brother in recognition of the funniest put-down of the day so far.

'Seriously, though,' said Callum, once he'd finally regained his composure, 'you need to sort your hair out. You look like Mum after the time we put glue in her shampoo!'

Now it was Adam's turn to get gross with the toast. It sprayed all over the kitchen floor as he doubled over at the memory of that day.

'Her face!' He howled with laughter as he played the moment back in his mind. 'When she opened the bathroom door – her *hair* – I've never seen anyone so shocked!'

'Oh, not shocked,' his mum corrected him, '*furious*. Which is exactly what I'll be in five seconds' time if you don't get a move on!'

They had fifteen minutes before they would be marked as being officially late for school, and Mum had one hour and fifteen minutes before she'd be late for work, so Adam knew they weren't really in any serious danger. But Mum never saw it that way. All Mum saw was the multiple things that could go wrong to slow them down on their way.

Like, for instance, their car, which today took five attempts to splutter to life before choking to a standstill at the end of the road.

The false start reminded Adam to dig in his pocket, fish out the 40p change from yesterday's lunch money and pop it into the cardboard box he'd wedged between the two front seats three months ago. It was a shoebox, with the lid taped on, a coin slot cut into

the top and the words 'New Gearbox Fund' scrawled across it in purple marker pen.

They'd only had the car for four months, after their old car – the beloved 'Dadmobile' – was stolen from outside their house. Mum thought she'd found a real bargain with the used Ford Focus. The ad had read – '*New tyres, new brakes, new gearbox!*' so she spent every last penny on it. Sadly, after getting the car home, she discovered that the advert hadn't listed all the things the car *had*, it was a list of all the things the car *needed*.

A new gearbox was right at the top of that list, but, at six hundred pounds, they were a loooooong way from being able to afford it. Luckily Adam had the problem under control — so far his 'New Gearbox Fund' idea had raised a whopping twelve pounds and twenty pence!

'Listen to all that money!' Adam gasped in mock amazement as he gave the box a shake. 'Not long to go now, Mum! This time in three years we'll be halfway saved up!'

'Adam, don't even joke,' his mum groaned, knowing he was probably right. 'I've had enough of this horrible old banger!'

It was a sentence that Adam struggled to make sense of. OK, he knew that, to Mum, a 'banger' was an out-of-date, unreliable car, like the Ford Focus they were sitting in, which was two years older than Adam, and was presently making a noise like an asthmatic donkey. But to Adam, a 'banger' was YouTube slang for a video that was an unstoppable, runaway, viral mega-hit. In Adam's mind a 'banger' was an amazing thing, not something that could ever be used in the same sentence as the words 'horrible' and 'old'.

And a 'banger' was what he was watching right now. (Or trying to watch – his phone was almost as useless as their car. It was bashed and beaten, with a camera that barely worked, and was five models out of date. But Adam was grateful for it, all the same. He knew his mum struggled to pay the six-pound bill every month, but he made sure it was money well spent.

His phone was a window to another world, a window that he gazed through for hours each day, where no matter how down, or stressed, or worried he was feeling, there was always someone like him – another world-class-cheerer-upper – uploading content that would put a smile back on Adam's face. Through the window of his phone he could escape to the land of TikTok, surf the waters of Instagram, and, best of all, explore the endless realms of YouTube – a place where he dreamed he might one day migrate to and become a fully certified citizen. To be a YouTuber was Adam's greatest dream – a dream where he could follow in the footsteps of all his favourite YouTubers and deliver his cheering-up skills not just to his mum and Callum, but to *millions* of people across the globe. *Just imagine making that many people happy*, he marvelled to himself.)

His favourite YouTuber, Ed Almighty, had posted a new video overnight, and even though Adam could only watch a few seconds at a time between bufferings, it was still one of the funniest things he had ever seen.

'I seriously don't understand what all the hype is about that guy,' groaned Callum, trying to lean himself forward from the back seat enough to see Adam's stuttering screen. 'He's so overrated. He didn't deserve *any* of those awards he got at WebCon last year!'

For the online community, WebCon was like the Oscars. It was where every web-fan like Adam dreamed of going. Adam would have especially loved to go last year, when Ed Almighty was the star of the show. Callum wasn't a massive fan of Ed Almighty. He was more into Jack-OJ.

Adam thought they were *both* heroes.

'Adam, you could be a better YouTuber than Ed Almighty without even trying! I'm not even joking!'

'Ha!' Adam laughed as he reached a hand back to give Callum an affectionate hair-ruffle, like he was an obedient puppy. 'You're a good little brother, Callum, you know that? Yesh you are! Yesh you *are*! Who's a good boy? You are!'

While Adam appreciated Callum's compliment, he knew that Callum was very, very wrong about him. Sure, Adam would have loved to be a YouTuber. There was nothing in the world he wanted to do more! That's what that glue-shampoo prank on his mum had been all about – it was practice! He and Callum had made *dozens* of YouTube videos. But that's all they ever were – 'practice' videos, which sat on Adam's hard drive and had never even so much as sniffed the bandwidth of a journey to the realms of YouTube.

The dream was never going to happen, and Adam knew it. And it wasn't just because his ancient laptop took all night to upload a five-minute video, and it wasn't because the camera on his brick of a phone was half dead. It was because there was something about Adam that Callum didn't know. Something that Adam didn't *want* Callum to know. A 'secondary school something'. Something that, if he ever found it out, would change Callum's opinion of Adam forever. And now that Callum was in his last year of primary school, and would join Adam's secondary school next year, Adam knew it was only a matter of time before his secret came out.

About the Author and Illustrator

Adam B is a household name. Not only hugely popular online, with his videos boasting more than a billion views overall, Adam is also an experienced live-television host and was previously a presenter on the world's longest-running kids' TV programme, *Blue Peter*. Adam's debut novel, *Adam Wins the Internet*, in which he encouraged readers to aspire to achieve their dreams, was published by Bloomsbury in 2022. This is his second phenomenally funny, out-of-this-world adventure.

James Lancett is a London-based illustrator, director and yellow-sock lover! He is known for his illustrations for *Lightning Girl* by Alesha Dixon, the Avengers Assembly graphic novels, the Max Einstein series by James Patterson, and many others.